THE DISAPPEARING ACT

ALSO BY MARIA STEPANOVA
FROM NEW DIRECTIONS

Holy Winter 20/21

In Memory of Memory

MARIA STEPANOVA

The Disappearing Act

translated by Sasha Dugdale

A NEW DIRECTIONS PAPERBOOK ORIGINAL

Manufactured in the United States of America
First published as New Directions Paperbook 1653 in 2026

Library of Congress Cataloging-in-Publication Data
Names: Stepanova, Mariia author | Dugdale, Sasha translator
Title: The disappearing act / Maria Stepanova ;
translated by Sasha Dugdale.
Other titles: Fokus. English
Description: New York : New Directions Publishing Corporation, 2026.
Identifiers: LCCN 2025049749 | ISBN 9780811239400 paperback |
ISBN 9780811239417 ebook
Subjects: LCSH: Expatriate authors—Fiction | Women authors,
Russian—Fiction | LCGFT: Autobiographical fiction | Novels | Fiction
Classification: LCC PG3488.T4755 F6513 2026
LC record available at https://lccn.loc.gov/2025049749

10 9 8 7 6 5 4 3 2 1

New Directions Books are published for James Laughlin
by New Directions Publishing Corporation
80 Eighth Avenue, New York

THE DISAPPEARING ACT

1.

In the summer of 2023 the grass carried on growing as if nothing at all was wrong. It grew as if that was simply how things had to be, as if to demonstrate once again that, no matter how much killing took place on the face of the earth, the grass at least intended to keep on stubbornly pushing up through the soil. Perhaps it was a duller green than usual, perhaps it lost the milk-white tinge of its tips almost immediately, but still it grew on undeterred. Almost as if the lack of water forced the grass to cling tighter to the earth, sending out ever-newer shoots that dried and withered before they could reach their full growth.

In the summer of 2023 the planet experienced its hottest day since records began. Picture the scene: generations of Lilliputian scientists pressing themselves against Earth's vast body, measuring her temperature day and night, gathering samples of the sweat at her brow and taking particular pleasure in noting the parts of her that were coldest. All this information they recorded in a logbook, presumably finding consolation in the steady breathing of the sleeping giant; the way in which extraordinary rushes of fever and chills were quickly followed by what might be called normal temperatures; or the condition of her hair and nails, which was as good as could be expected for someone who had lain motionless through the ages, allowing others to do with her as they wished. Perhaps long ago she had shifted into a very different state of mind, one in which she was no longer provoked to anger or dismay by our actions, and now feels herself to be a star, pierced through with fire and already smoldering; or a swath of cloth, boundless and featureless, indifferent to everything, like a stage curtain in the darkness. Or, who knows, perhaps she's amused by the way we assume nothing new will ever come of her, that we continue to expect our daily and yearly deliveries of milk and honey like children expecting breakfast, yawning children who scramble to the kitchen and wait for their mother to put bowls of yogurt or cornflakes on the table in front of them. But what if the bowls suddenly contained scorpions, or writhing grubs, or bluebottles? What if the thermostat was turned right up, so the kitchen was stiflingly hot, or what if frogs rained down from the sky, slapping against the windows? What if a plague on the firstborn began? This is a game that can be kept going for a good while, especially if it begins with almost imperceptible changes: the grass that withers a little early, or the trains that seem to forget the timetable, delayed for hours, or else rushing ahead with preternatural speed, only then to stand silent on a wide plain, waiting for their allotted arrival time.

It was on such a train that the novelist, who went by the name of M, sat waiting, wondering just how late she was going to be. The yellowing fields outside, the net on the seatback with an empty Coke bottle jammed into it, even the occupant of the seat next to hers—all were portents of a delay she could not avoid. Trains now behaved as if they were living creatures, free from human control; all one could do was hope for their good will, although it was unclear how or even whether this differed from the good will of humans. Ticket inspectors had all but disappeared from the trains, and no one seemed to care any longer; you could go a long way without having to show a ticket.

Still, the novelist M, who was traveling from one country to another, confidently expected to arrive at her destination, if not on this train then at least on another. She was armed with a ticket and a seat reservation, and she'd picked up an avocado sandwich from one of the more upmarket station kiosks where the bread was fresh and the coffee strong. She'd once heard that an action only needed to be repeated twelve times for a new and enduring habit to be formed. For example, if, after a day's work, you were to go to a café with a river view and drink a simple glass of white wine then on the thirteenth evening, the habit would suddenly manifest itself, like the head of a seal emerging from the water, and you'd be a new and different person: the sort of person who sits sipping wine in the evening, without really knowing why, waiting for the new words that fit this new life like a glove, and that will in time appear in your mouth together with the taste of wine.

In any case, as M sometimes reflected, they say that the human body has a habit of replacing all its cells with new ones every seven years. After seven years you wake up a completely different person without even noticing and only continue to think of yourself as a familiar and predictable creature because you aren't paying attention. But then again, she wondered, turning away from the occupant of the seat next to hers with his expanse of newspaper, and looking grumpily out of the window, could one really call this behavior a genuine *habit*, when in most cases the human body doesn't manage to renew itself the full twelve times. By the thirteenth you'd be over ninety, a rare achievement for the human organism, and at that age a person is facing inevitable transformation into a handful of ashes in an urn, or a box whose contents we'd prefer not to think about.

She'd certainly passed through the city's main station twelve or more times. So her desire to join the morning line for coffee and a paper bag filled with something warm and nourishing (and from one particular kiosk) could by now be considered a habit rather than a passing whim; and she herself looked like a woman who knew what she wanted, placing her paper cup decisively into its carton tray and pressing on the correct lid. For M, who hadn't lived in this city long, precision of movement and the knowledge of one's future trajectory (the underpass to platform five for northbound trains and platform one for southbound) had a particular importance, as if guaranteeing that she had a place both on the waiting train and the journey towards it, as well as in the new life itself, to which she had not yet been entirely reconciled.

Judging by the number of times she'd had to travel somewhere and work "as a novelist" in different cities and countries and then travel back, pulling her light suitcase easily from the luggage rack each time, then she clearly did have a place in this new life, many places in fact, and in each one people wanted to ask her about the books she had once written; and then, with far more curiosity, about the country she'd come from. This country was currently waging war against a neighboring country, killing the inhabitants with missiles, with fire from the skies, with bare hands, and yet it still couldn't conquer it, nor accept that its opponent was not going to offer itself up on a plate.

Sometimes—fairly frequently, in fact—this country of hers also found time to kill its own inhabitants, seeming to consider them as nothing more than mutinous body parts that had become dangerous distractions from the acts of hunting and feeding. The foreign city where M now lived was full of people fleeing from both countries, and those who'd been attacked by her own compatriots regarded their former neighbors with horror and suspicion, as if life before the war had ceased to have any meaning and had simply masked a similarity with the devouring beast.

Many of the people who were native to this foreign city wanted to know more about this beast, not simply to protect themselves from its repulsive maw, but also because big predators interest us, we herbivores, who find it hard to understand where such violence comes from and how it functions. They interrogated the novelist M on the beast's habits with a sort of anxious compassion, as if she too had been bitten, even half-swallowed, and the fact she had been left lying in the grass, relatively untouched, was only an accident. Some wanted to know how it was possible that the beast hadn't yet been killed or hadn't consumed itself in its unbounded greed, and these people hinted that M and those she knew in her country should have taken measures against it long before the beast grew to its present size and began consuming everyone.

M absolutely agreed with this, but she found it hard to explain that the very nature of the beast made it tricky to hunt down or to fight. You see, she might have reasoned, it's not as if the beast was there in front of me, or even behind me. No, it was all around me, and to such an extent that it's taken me years to realize that I was living inside it, that I was perhaps even born inside it. Do you remember the story, she continued to herself silently, about the old man and the wooden boy, sitting inside a sea monster with only a stump of tallow candle? They could have caused the monster some discomfort by, say, jumping up and down in its belly or by making a fire. But in our case the disproportionate size of the beast means you can do it no real harm, let alone kill it. The only hope is that one day it will begin to choke and puke, and, without knowing how it happened, you suddenly find yourself on the outside, seeing quite distinctly that the room you spent so long in was in fact its stomach. It so happened that I was a part of a beast, if only because I was swallowed accidentally, or grew up inside it by mistake. I understand this means my experience is flawed and my account hardly reliable. Still, if necessary, I am willing to report on the internal fixings of the creature, a creature I left only recently for dry land.

2.

M now lived in a place overrun with beasts (as well as birds, and among those birds, herons flying low over the lake, so you could clearly see the elegance of their weightless construction) and people who had, it seemed, very little understanding of what one might expect from such beasts. Once when a fox attacked and killed a local swan right in front of the children playing in the lakeside grass, the fox's shamelessness was discussed at the communal dinner table and someone gave the opinion that its behavior was unacceptable and that something should be done about it. M had no idea how one could prevent a fox from expressing its inner beast and refrained from joining the conversation, fearing she might appear too closely acquainted with the morals of those who ate the living without caring who saw them.

And yet even here there were people who who saw things for what they were and took precautions. She was once having a guilty smoke on a bench hidden behind some bushes when a small gray-haired woman emerged from the thicket and demanded to know what M was doing there. She looked official, if a little disheveled; she wore a fitted uniform, a sort of shiny boiler suit with epaulettes, and indeed she immediately produced identification, a card sealed in cellophane that was already coming unstuck in the damp. M had nothing to show her in turn, except the cigarette, but there must have been something in the novelist's look that testified to her trustworthiness, and the woman in the uniform immediately began treating her as a potential ally. She was, it seemed, a guardian of the swans that swam from one lake to another, bringing up their young, and astonishing passersby with their titanic grandeur and whiteness; she hadn't just been sitting in the thicket, she'd been keeping watch. She was, she explained, no lone ranger but part of a mighty force of swan watchers who kept guard day and night on the lakes; uniformed volunteers and activists who lay sleepless in hideouts waiting for a predator to attempt to harm the welfare of the giant birds. There were forty, all told, she said, puffing out her chest and allowing M to examine a plastic wallet containing a collection of dirty swan feathers.

There was something in the manner of Jay Jay (as the woman had asked to be called) that suggested she had in fact no colleagues and that she guarded the lakes alone, despite the references to her fellow keepers and the help that would swiftly arrive should anything happen. She knew how to deal with foxes: there was no point in offering them dog food (although they never turned down cat food) but their favorite snack was a hardboiled egg. "People, though, are another matter," she said, looking at M as if she knew something about her, too. People stole eggs from the swans' nests—who knew for what purpose, perhaps for use in occult ritual. "Yes, there's nothing *people* wouldn't do," she repeated grimly. "A month ago now we found babies—two babies," she said, translating her words into English, "with knife wounds all over their bellies." "Goodness," M squeaked. "What did you do, get the police?" "No," replied the woman sadly. "They were quite dead. We buried them. Two beautiful specimens, hardly even in their first plumage."

M saw Jay Jay a few times more circling the lakes, sometimes on a bicycle, sometimes on foot, wearing a neon vest over the boiler suit. Once M even tried to report to her a kingfisher she'd seen a day or two before, but Jay Jay was unexpectedly brusque, as if she'd learnt something new about humankind, or even about the novelist herself.

Long-distance trains were a space where humans found themselves in unusual proximity, albeit not as wearyingly tightly pressed as on a crowded platform or on the metro. But in a crowd you at least know that it will soon come to an end and, because you share the space not with a singular other but with a multitude of others who resemble you, it takes a conscious effort to single out any particular person from that crowd, to look properly at them, to consider them for more than a moment. Far easier not to; to use that special absentminded gaze that registers only distance and movement, the millimeters of air between you and another person's shoulder, and how everyone is crushed together by the movement of the train, or how the mass of people begins to strain towards the doors as the station approaches.

But in intercity trains you know you'll almost certainly have to spend long hours shoulder to shoulder with another. Of course you can hope that your carriage will be empty, and the seat beside you, too. Then you can put your jacket and bag on it as if it is yours by rights, as if you have drawn a blind down and only the ticket inspector can look into your lair. Here you are free—no one can reach you—to eat your avocado sandwich and drink your water without looking up from your book, or sleep with your legs outstretched, or sit and watch those around you with vague enmity, as if wearing a cloak of invisibility so you can stare at anyone without inhibition.

Such a cloak had featured in a certain French book that M had once greatly loved. M was just over thirty when she read the book, and the heroine was around fifty, and this fact alone was consoling, like a dress made to grow into. There it was: you could change your life utterly at the age of fifty and start afresh in a way you could never have foreseen. One evening, the heroine, standing outside a house in the suburbs, sees her husband kissing another woman under a streetlamp. The woman was younger, more capable of arousing desire, as one might say. At this point events take a turn: our heroine waits until her husband goes on a short business trip and while he's away she sells her parents' house, where the couple had been living, as well as the furniture, the Bechsteins; she gives away her own books and clothes and packs his shirts and razor into a suitcase to send to his workplace. Then she disappears so entirely she can never be found again. She avoids using bank cards, throws away her cell phone so her movements can't be traced, and takes circuitous routes, one bus ride after another, going wherever her mood takes her. In every new city she gets rid of the clothes she is wearing and changes the color of her hair or her hat, and keeps on traveling. The only thing she can't do is leave Europe, as she would have to show her passport at the border. But she visits the northern lakes, then the Mediterranean islands. She gradually becomes used to a new sensation of security, for which she needs no house or apartment, nor even a roof over her head. Now all she needs to hide herself is a fissure in a cliff wall where she can shelter from the rain. Or a hooded cloak that she could draw down over her eyes. Or her own eyelids that she can lower in order to see nothing more of the world.

When the life of the novelist M changed (and it did so without her active involvement or even her agreement) she was also around fifty, but she was still waiting for the moment when she could close her eyes and that would be enough to feel at home in the world. It was clearly much harder than the book made it seem, and the cloak itself was not reliable. The seat next to hers was occupied by a man who obviously had the same feeling of suppressed awkwardness, and their conjoined suffering could only be addressed by one of those well-disposed but fast-drying conversations, or by making it immediately clear that an invisible wall separated them both so neither could see or hear the other, and then gazing intently out of the window as if the scenery was deeply compelling. In such circumstances eating the avocado sandwich would give her no pleasure—the packaging would rustle, the crumbs would scatter on her lap, and it would somehow encroach on her neighbor's silence and estrangement.

The novelist's neighbor was perhaps traveling on business: he wore a fitted gray suit despite the warm weather. The suit had clearly been chosen with an air-conditioned office in mind, and you could tell he felt constricted in it and that the journey ahead was long. M stared unblinkingly out at the landscape (the windmills turning on the pale hills, the horses standing in fields with their heads down examining the grass, and beyond them plains and agricultural land) and tried to guess what her companion did for a living. She felt for some reason that he must work in insurance or be a salesman for air-conditioning units, journeying from town to town just as she did, until it had long ceased feeling like real travel at all. The best moment in the day was when you entered the hotel room, hung your jacket on a plastic hanger and fell backwards onto the bedspread in your shirt and trousers, staring briefly at the ceiling before closing your eyes, knowing you still had to get back up, fold your work trousers on the back of the chair so they didn't crease, maybe have a beer in the hotel bar, and call home before turning in for the night.

M's life, in its present iteration, had much in common with the life of her fellow traveler. Perhaps the single difference was that she, when she entered her hotel room, opened and sorted the contents of her suitcase, shaking out each item before hanging it in the wardrobe, placing the books in a pile on the desk, as if she were staying for a long time and was going to be using the desk for writing. She had decided on this routine the year before and she'd done it ever since, even if she was only spending a few hours of the night in the room. She could no longer recall the original significance of this fastidious imitation of order—but for a number of reasons her life now had a slightly salty taste, requiring small spoons of sugar to make it more or less digestible, and this little routine was one such sweetener, along with a promise that on every trip she would do something for herself: a walk around the botanical gardens with their rose bushes and beds of aconites, or even just late checkout and a lie-in till noon between hotel sheets.

If M could have spoken with the younger version of herself, the self of fifteen years before, perhaps, she would have found it hard to justify all this. For the younger M, life in a foreign country and the endless traveling from city to city would not just have been delightful opportunities to look about her and take in sights, but an education she felt sorely in need of. She had a low opinion of herself, but allowed that the formless material of her being should be given the chance to shape itself and improve. If there was something that annoyed her about the way she was, it was not her lack of education and the resulting awkwardness, both of word and gesture—it was her slowness. She was growing up, improving, so unbearably slowly, and experiencing only at thirty or forty the milestones in her development you might expect of a three-year-old. She never seemed to reach the point when she could say for sure that she was functioning with the full force nature had unleashed in her. She hardly considered her writings to be work, seeing them akin to notches made on a doorframe, as you might mark a child's height on their fourth birthday. But her ability to think, to understand and to draw conclusions was important for her, and she'd wanted to believe that with age she was growing stronger in this regard, so that one day she might reach a stage of deeper understanding, especially if she traveled the world and kept her eyes and ears open.

Yet over the last year and a half M seemed hardly to have grown at all, just as sometimes a fetus stops developing in the indifferent womb. She had also lost all belief in her ability to make considered judgments. Her thoughts were rapid and jerky, extending no further than a short piece of elastic on which a plush monkey might dangle and bounce—at best they were mere statements of fact: this water is cold, this tea is hot. She knew it was vital to hold such brief statements apart; whenever they touched they began to spark and led to a sort of short internal outage, as when at school she'd been asked to divide a number by zero.

Take the beast, and the war which began because of the beast. There was a time when M was still in charge of her life, or thought she was, and understanding the workings of the beast was, back then, of the utmost importance to her. She'd gathered some knowledge and a series of observations to this end and had been attempting to analyze the beast's habits and its possible intentions—but it was growing, you might say, in parallel with her and she was barely able to note it all down. It was not as if M had thought of this as her main occupation—in fact she was interested in quite different things: mostly the stories of other people, which she collected like postage stamps, attempting to arrange them on paper in their single correct order. Most of these stories, it must be said, did have some direct connection with the beast, however it seemed as if this belonged to the past—after all, in these more enlightened times no one rips off another's head for no reason, or only very, very rarely. M remembered a story she'd heard in company. A girl had dreamed that she'd been sent by her family to the beast to be devoured; everyone was terribly upset, her mother advised her to distract the beast with chatter until it fell asleep, as that might work for the first night at least. "But the strangest thing," said the dreamer, "was when they came for me and led me away, I realized that this had been the whole point of my life, its hidden plan, if you considered it without frills or qualifiers, user profiles on Tinder or PhDs in philosophy. It transpired that I was put on this earth to be eaten, like some battery hen: born in a cage, shitting on its own feet and leaving the world plucked, frozen and wrapped in plastic. And so I barely even resisted, because what's the point in resisting one's higher destiny?"

Today, M, sitting on the train and approaching the town of G, where she would catch a connecting train, remembered that episode with distinct displeasure. Like a hopeful child, she had always, until recently, held an implicit trust in the universe, that it was watching over her and her development—just as one trusts handrails before a sudden precipitous fall down the stairs. Maybe she'd been proceeding slowly, with the delays and changes in direction one might associate with a railway journey, but she was at least moving towards the fulfilment of a task, even if it was only the meaningless formation of self. Now it suddenly seemed to her that the whole grand process of growth and feeding resembled the chicken factory or the cattle yard, where you are lovingly tended until you reach the necessary weight. She was used to thinking of herself as a work in progress, a slightly more mature grammar schoolgirl, waiting for graduation or a successful match, but today it seemed obvious that the inevitable conclusion was a cleaver and a package of meat. It made no difference what was preparing you for the finale, whether it was the beast you were watching from a hide, or something else far larger: the end result was clear as day, and all she wanted now was to sit motionless, for a long time, pretending to be dead.

3.

M's spoon of sugar, a good-sized spoon to sweeten this particular trip, was the traveling itself: a connecting train would take her from the town of G into another peaceable country, and the journey entailed six quiet hours on a train, during which time she would be entirely cut off from life. For that interval it would be as if she didn't exist; no one would have the right to buttonhole her, to insist on a conversation. It is thought (and this is a great blessing) that a person on a journey is occupied with a form of work that requires maximum concentration, and has the right not to answer calls or letters; quite as if a traveler lives for that brief moment in an opaque capsule with a "do not disturb" sign on it, and interrupting her is simply not permitted.

M had counted on this period of invisibility while hardly believing it might come to pass. She was now a novelist in name only as she wasn't actually writing anything, nor had any future plan to do so. Or perhaps you might say she was a novelist "on occasion"—and the occasion was usually at the end of one of these journeys, when readers gathered to meet her and talk. Not all of them were *her* readers, those who read her books and wanted to ask questions about them, but everyone was undoubtedly part of a community that loved and understood letters in the right order on a page, and believed that a conversation with an author would open to the reader a kind of little door in a paper wall. In the country where M currently resided, these conversations were even a tradition of sorts. In the country of her birth, the audience at a literary event was mainly composed of those who already knew an author's texts and wanted to hear the author reading or talking about the work; but here, a "meet the author" event was more like a bride show—people came along blindly, in the strange hope that the woman sitting at a low table with two bottles of water on it would give them grounds to fall in love with her, that she would say or do something to make them buy her book and spend time engaging with her words alone, without an intermediary. Sometimes such things could happen, but in any case, M liked the way audiences gathered to hear about the purpose and the subject of a piece of writing, and how they never lost their belief that they might just hear something new, something vital for them. She didn't just like it, it touched her inexplicably and at such moments she was prepared to be a novelist once again, even if, in fact, all she was doing was recounting some old stories or thinking aloud, and really there should have been another name for this occupation.

She had no plans to write anything in the six hours of solitude she had been granted that day, in a seat some kind people had reserved for her, as she'd requested: the single seat at the end of the carriage with no one sitting beside her. It wasn't that she had nothing to do, quite the opposite, she had far too many uncompleted tasks, each pinching her like a clothespin, never letting her forget it, so she hardly knew where to start. But she had a plan, and just as soon as she changed trains, and the scenery was flashing past the window once again, she would get on with work.

In the house by the lake where she now lived, and to which she would soon return, if you went out onto the balcony at dusk, in the summer, you could often hear from the far side of the lake, and beyond a thick screen of trees, the sudden playing of horns, as if from a barracks or a bandstand in a park. It was never a whole tune, played from start to finish, only the opening, haunting notes, repeated several times as if they were always on the point of continuing but never doing so. In her childhood, in the country of her birth, which was then called something different, she'd been sent to pioneer camp and remembered such sounds, which were used as the reveille or the call to assembly. What followed never fulfilled the promise that sounded so powerfully in those long high notes. Here in this foreign town the music resounded even more grandly, but it wasn't clear who it was summoning: other people who understood its meaning and knew what delights it promised, or, incidentally but no less urgently, M herself, regardless of the disgrace and the hopelessness of her situation. Now the sound came almost every evening, giving her the restless notion that something must be undertaken or completed before it was too late.

Her plan was very simple, it required neither preparation nor time, but for some reason she was never able to carry it out in the place she now called home, even though every day she set out to try. Her affairs, both practical and spiritual, had by that time reached such a state of disorder that it was impossible to deal with them without devising some kind of system: clear some tasks out of the mind, like rotten fruit from the fridge, place others in order of importance quickly and decisively and so make time for the most important, the as yet undecided affair, which would take space and stillness to resolve.

It was not just that she had to recall all her duties and unfulfilled obligations and set them down, both on paper and in her head, although that was the main practical part of the operation. M hoped that somewhere along the way, at least by the end of the process, when all her thoughts had been put in order, she would attain a higher clarity (a clarity of a higher *caliber*, she might once have said, but that word's association with weaponry brought the beast back to mind along with the thought of who was being destroyed in that instant). It sounded strange but she wanted to find out who she was now, what she wanted to do with herself, what she might be transformed into—because she had forgotten how to be who she was.

It had reached the point where none of the tasks and jobs she had given herself in this new life, however small or undemanding, had been completed, despite her having always been a generally reliable and responsible person. And it wasn't because she'd forgotten how to do things, like answering letters or composing the texts she'd promised to deliver; she remembered well how to do all these, and never felt as if she'd lost her ability to do them. It was just that in order to begin and complete even one item on the endless list of obligations, she had to bring together two vast tectonic plates in her head, bring them into line so they clicked into place, and M would suddenly know who she was, and at last feel the ground under her feet. But this never happened, the jigsaw puzzle remained unsolved, the smashed blue china cup could not be glued together, and her long and monotonous thought processes always brought her back to the dreary realization that once again there was no one to do her work for her.

Whoever M had or hadn't become, there were some constant elements in her life. As soon as she began searching for the right words, for any words, she had the sensation of a mouse in her mouth, and she couldn't for the life of her spit the creature out. The mouse wriggled, alive and trapped between her teeth, and she wasn't sure whether she should simply bite down, killing it with a crunch, or just carry on living with it in her mouth, unable to think beyond its presence.

And so the novelist M was unable to do anything of use, and even her conversations were conducted over the soundless squealing of a mouse, as she fought her rising nausea and clutched at the arms of the chair she sat in. Her life now boiled down to reading the news and military dispatches, each worse than the last, the rising numbers of dead and displaced, the children and pets in bomb shelters sitting on outspread raincoats and anoraks, the burnt-out buildings on wastelands, and old women with nowhere to go—while M simply sat there.

And yet today she had hopes of sorting through the contents of her head like a box of old documents, throwing away the unneeded papers and organizing what was left into neat piles. It wasn't the first time she had performed this act of mental hygiene, and the process had always given her the clarity she needed. The hero in a famous old book called this mental activity "laundering," but for M it was more like ironing: steaming and pressing flat all the internal wrinkles and creases that would otherwise become engrained, hardened, and might even hurt any careless fingers picking through them. Until recently, it had worked, her thoughts had ordered themselves into neat soldierly rows (here she shuddered at the image and rewound a little). Her thoughts, she began again, started acting in a reasonable fashion, kept their place in line and didn't suddenly crowd in one direction, filling the aisles and crushing anyone who had fallen underfoot in the stampede. However, everything had changed, and in the house by the lake she'd spent long hours trying to persuade herself to sit down at her desk and begin anew. And always, to her irritation and relief, a letter would arrive that she simply had to answer, or someone would call her out of the blue, summoning her to the other side of town to meet up with friends, or something else happened *there*, far away, and so she would sit with the computer on her lap, endlessly refreshing the news until her eyes went dim. But now, now, in the quiet carriage, there was no escape and she fully intended to force herself to sit and think everything through and leave the train with the feeling that the journey had not been in vain.

The train began to move again, at last approaching the town of G, where she had exactly eighteen minutes to catch her next train. Her neighbor had long ago put away his laptop and got down his bag (a sporty rucksack that didn't quite go with the suit) and was now hovering by the toilet at the end of the carriage as if he feared he wouldn't manage to disembark in time and would be left on the train. M reached for her suitcase, but there was no longer any room in the aisle, so she stood looking over her seatback at the other passengers waiting. Just in front of her was a tall man with fair hair and broad shoulders. She'd noticed him when she got on the train as he was strikingly good-looking—a scrubbed-clean, even-featured face, with gray eyes and a strong chin: one of those men she was simply not destined for, and whenever she encountered them she would begin stammering and making mistakes in English. From here she could study his back, as well as his hair, drawn into a tidy ponytail at the nape, with a series of discreet hair clips in a neat row, keeping all the usually wayward little nape hairs in place—an indication of the control he exerted over his appearance. It pleased her to gaze at him: even though the man was someone else's source of pleasure and not hers, she refused to let his inaccessibility upset her—she had far too many other reasons for a grief she kept constantly in check.

A little further ahead was a boy in a red cap, an eager grin on his flushed face. He was glancing around, looking out at the approaching platform, obviously hoping to see someone on it, and it was clear that given the opportunity he'd have stuck his head out of the window, or even jumped through it. Ahead of him was a woman holding a tiny fluffy lapdog and M suddenly dreamed she had her own dog—one like that, or perhaps quite different—and when she ate her breakfast her dog would take its place under the table, pressing with its whole body against her leg so it too could partake of the human meal. Now the train was slowing, and soon came smoothly to a complete standstill.

The station was huge, dark, made of wrought iron and glass; it reminded her so much of an old aviary in a park that she had the immediate desire to fly up under its arches and hang in the air, wings whirring like a pigeon's. The boy in the cap was met by a sleepy-looking girl, her cheeks almost as pink as her hair. The man with the ponytail disappeared into the crowd. M rolled her light wheelie bag towards the departures board. If she had a dog, the novelist continued to think, it would come to her at night, clattering its claws across the parquet, and curl up with a contented sigh by her legs.

But this was strange: her connecting train didn't seem to exist. A different train stood at the platform indicated on her ticket, an empty double-decker, clearly not departing anytime soon. This was in itself was unremarkable, even predictable—but there was nothing on the departures board, bright with lit-up numbers and names of towns, to tell M where to go or what to do. Slightly anxious now, she quickened her pace, checking to her right and left, and already at a jog she hastened over to a glass kiosk marked "Information."

The girl in the kiosk was as calm as a park at dusk. She took M's ticket to study it and M noticed that her hands were covered in a complicated tattoo of two colors, and along each finger ran curling tendrils of ink, like roses climbing a trellis. M stared, then shook herself and looked away. "Your train's been canceled, I'm afraid," said the girl placidly. "You'll get some compensation, of course."

"No!" squealed M, gesticulating and trying to explain all at once how she had to travel, she had to keep going, she was expected in another country for a reading that very evening. But the girl patiently replied that there was no way she could travel any further, there was a rail strike in the country she was traveling to, and all the trains were canceled, even into the night. Perhaps it would be worth looking into flights, she added, though she could not help with that.

Standing by the glass kiosk, clutching her suitcase and turned away from the crowds, M sent the organizers of the foreign festival an email, then a text, then a voicemail. She looked about her gloomily—the station was teeming, it was Friday, already the weekend had begun and people were traveling home or to their parents, moving in every possible direction. It was hot, and all of a sudden she realized that she had left the avocado sandwich she'd been looking forward to eating in the net pocket on the seatback in the train; it was now out of reach and rushing away from her at a speed the novelist M could only aspire to.

4.

By the kiosk selling refreshments, with its short line, M was waylaid by a homeless man, barefoot and wearing a transparent raincoat, under which his jutting collarbones were sharply visible. She had by then managed to order a coffee and a sandwich, exactly like the last one, and the paper packet lay on the counter, whetting her appetite and promising a full stomach. "Buy me some food too, please," the man began repeating insistently, but in such a low tone she could hardly make out what he was saying, especially as she hardly spoke the language. She stared at him, uncomprehendingly, as he spoke again: "Some food, please. Buy me some food."

M hurriedly replied, "Yes, yes, of course," and turned to the woman at the counter to request another sandwich. "No," said the homeless man. "I want cheesecake. Cheesecake," he repeated very distinctly, "this one here." "OK, cheesecake," she repeated after him, "this one here." And she pointed her finger at the glass as he had done. The woman raised her eyebrows but placed a piece of cheesecake in a bag with a few paper napkins. "There," said M placatingly and reached for her own cup of coffee. The man in the raincoat was gone in an instant, groping in the paper bag as he went, and M was just thinking she should have bought him a coffee as he'd have nothing to wash it down with, when another man appeared in front of her, similar to the last—not in age or appearance, but in the aura of hopelessness he exuded, as palpable as an odor. He was dressed and shod after a fashion, and under his arm he held a length of floral material, a curtain perhaps, on which he'd clearly been sleeping, its dirty hem dragging along the concrete. He looked at her, but in an odd manner, finding a point between her eyebrows to focus on, so she couldn't catch his gaze.

"Buy me something to eat," he said with the same intonation as the first man, as if someone had schooled them in what to say and how to say it. M mumbled a reply, pushed her bag with the sandwich into his hands and walked quickly to the station exit without looking back.

Outside now, her right hand seemed to remember all by itself that it was holding a cup of coffee and lifted it to her mouth. M began gulping it down, screwing her eyes up in the sunlight and gripping the wheelie bag with her left hand. People were walking along the street in both directions. Yellow taxis flashed by. A pigeon pecked at a crust of baguette. M took a deep breath and checked her cell phone: the festival hadn't answered her yet. She had to do something, something to occupy herself, so without too much thought she set off, turning to the left of the station and passing a parking lot, a tram stop, a café, all the sorts of things you might find near a station. She knew no one in the town of G, and she had no clear idea of what she should do next. If it hadn't been for the suitcase, rattling through the gravel on four wheels, she might have gone to a museum, but that idea immediately seemed absurd to her, and even, for some reason, dangerous. She could of course go and look for a café to settle in, somewhere she could wait for the call and at last eat something. But instead she stood still and stared at her phone again, checked her empty inbox, then looked online to see whether she could find a flight to where she needed to be that evening. There were no flights. She looked up and saw she was standing on a street corner, a pedestrian light flashing green. The novelist M crossed the road and began looking all about her.

There was a surfeit of eating places along the street: a Turkish café, a beer bar, a pizzeria, all equally unwelcoming, and perhaps for that reason empty, so you couldn't tell whether they were actually open or not. Maybe they got livelier in the evening and this was a quiet time of the day, the only passersby hurrying to and from the station. One or two tables with ashtrays on them stood outside the Turkish café, appealing to those who wanted to sit in the sun and close their eyes. The café door was open and the tiled floor was worn. A glass counter where food was displayed was still bare—they hadn't started cooking yet. But on a plastic tray behind the counter was a dish of flatbreads, long and oval as lakes. M had the sudden realization that she was terribly tired. "I'd like tea, a cup of tea," she said with the intonation of the homeless man she had just encountered. "And one of these," she pointed her finger at the topmost flatbread, not knowing what to call it.

It was called a *börek*, or so she learned, and they cut it into six large pieces for her, so she felt obliged to try it. But her appetite had completely forsaken her and she could barely swallow the bread, which was no longer warm and had the salty taste of tears. Still, the tea was hot, of a rich brick-red color, and she drank the first cup and immediately asked for another. She was not entirely sure why she wasn't sitting outside, as she'd planned to do, but inside, where the space was divided into a number of open booths. Apart from her there were two other customers: an old man with a bushy moustache sitting by a wall right inside the café, and another who sat hidden by a newspaper in a far corner. M checked her email. Nothing.

How long was it since she'd last been in a foreign town without work or plans, and with no clear sense of why she was there and what she might do—in fact, had she ever been in this situation? M had the disagreeable habit of obsessively studying her destinations' famous sights long before she set out on her travels, and in the past, before any planned trip, she would compare all the guidebooks, picking out and jotting down the highlights. Upon arrival she would move from one such landmark to the next with a sense of delicious expectation, which was almost always satisfied, because after all what could possibly spoil it—an Egyptian obelisk was hardly likely to slip from the spot it had occupied for centuries in order to escape a meeting with a novelist. Of course you might say that in this way she deprived herself of the pleasure of spontaneity, of the chance event or unforeseen twist, but she did not place much value on such things. She preferred the reliable transition from promise to fulfilment, permitting neither changes of mind nor the sudden desire to see something quite different, something not featured in a guidebook. M had never envisaged a situation in which she wanted nothing whatsoever, and even in this new life she had continued to place little treats along her own route, like Easter eggs hidden in bushes for children to find: a concert in four months' time, a visit to a museum in an as yet unknown town—although right now the thought of a museum or any other tourist sight gave rise only to a distinct feeling of nausea.

Here, however, a town in which she'd only intended to spend exactly eighteen minutes, she felt an unexpected sense of bewilderment, as you might feel in a place you can't quite bring yourself to leave, even though no one seems to want you there. She probably should have paid her bill, gone back to the station and traveled home. She could have been back at the house by the lake in two or so hours, well before dusk, and could even have pretended that she'd never left, that she'd been there the whole time, sitting on the couch in the room with white walls. But doing this seemed to her both impossible and inexplicably painful, as if everything that had already happened meant nothing at all; as if any action could be erased and you could just go back to the beginning. If she had learned anything from the past year it was the certainty that one could only move forward. Time and space, and even she herself, were paused, frozen like a computer, and all she could do was sit there, her arms folded, and stare at the empty teacup.

Just then, embarrassing though it was to admit, she felt a sudden need to go to the toilet. She looked about her, considering whether to pull her suitcase along with her, given it contained all her essential possessions. Taking it with her was awkward and showed a lack of trust in the establishment in which she'd sought shelter, but leaving it by the table with the half-eaten *börek* would be tempting fate, and she might bring even more misfortune on herself. She hesitated, then carefully drew the bag against the wall, placing a chair in front of it to guard it. Then she made her way towards the door labelled "Ladies." The door wouldn't open, it must have been locked. "Upstairs," remarked the elderly man with the moustache in a tone of old-fashioned gallantry. "Go up the stairs. The toilets are working up there." The novelist hesitated, looked worriedly at her suitcase and then climbed the spiral staircase as she'd been instructed.

On the second floor the unprepossessing little street café presented quite a different face: here an ornate and gilded paradise of carpets and hookahs glimmered in the darkness. This, it seemed was the real heart of the establishment, lit up in the evenings and humming with life. The curtains were made of thick velvet and the armchairs had spiral legs—there was not a living soul around. Sitting in the toilet, M thought about the fate of her suitcase: how she would go back downstairs to find it gone. Like in that Swiss book, she thought, where the man loses his shoe, then his suitcase, then the keys to his car and finally himself. She'd look in vain under the table, then she'd ask the old man with a mustache and the young man without one, and then the police would arrive and hours of filling out documents and crime reports would begin. She'd never get to the reading and she'd have to either stay here, in the town of G, or take the evening train home. Actually, that was a valid point—did she have enough money for a room in a hotel? She had money, and the money was with her, in a white bag hanging on the handle of the toilet door. But the thought that she was about to lose everything, from the plastic wallet containing her passport to her spare white shirt, and that her life was about to change irrevocably, took hold of her to such an extent that she had to consciously shake it off, as a dog shakes its body after a swim and the drops of water fly around.

5.

The suitcase was there where she'd left it, behind the chair, untouched. M sat down beside it, amazed at the weight of calm that suddenly descended upon her. Her cell phone, which had lost charge during the journey, was plugged into the wall, accumulating its necessary energy again. The man with the newspaper paid and left, but she continued to sit there listlessly. There was still no word from the festival, but for some reason this no longer bothered her, in fact the thought that they had forgotten about her, or lost her, so to speak, was oddly consoling and gave her a soft sleepy feeling of warmth in her stomach. Her inbox was empty. She opened her apps: she hadn't posted anything herself for a long time, but she checked her social media many times a day, as if terrified she'd miss something, even though she knew exactly what she would see—photographs of people and dogs immersed in dirty bubbling water, making desperate attempts to save themselves; people in little boats, hollow-eyed with exhaustion, rescuing other people and dogs from the roofs of houses submerged in water. In one place, all the animals in a zoo had perished: all those creatures with their human names had been locked in cages and there was no way to save them. In the surrounding countryside farm dogs on chains had been drowned beside their kennels and bowls, unable to escape from the rising water. And all this was happening as M was traveling, sitting around in cafés—but happening far away in the country which had been attacked by the country she was born in. In the occupied territory there had been a decrepit hydroelectric power station built many decades ago, and it had been attacked and blown up so that the water had breached the dam, flooding the land all around. M suddenly seized the cold *börek* with both hands and began forcing it into her mouth, choking and blinking. At first she didn't notice the old man with a moustache standing by her table, patiently saying something to her.

He was asking, she realized, whether the food was good. M shook her head to clear her thoughts, and then replied with complete honesty that the tea was delicious. The old man nodded and without asking her permission he sat down at her table. "Where are you from?"

The novelist was evidently too weary by now to keep up the necessary façade of politeness. "I always thought," she replied slowly, "that people ask this question to let a foreigner know that they're foreign, that they don't look the same as everyone else, they make mistakes when they speak, and they aren't at home here. I realize you're just interested in where I've come from, especially because the station is nearby. But that is what the question means to me."

"Well," said the man, "They've been asking me the same thing for forty years—as long as I've lived here. Better get used to it."

M had no intention of getting used to anything of the sort; however, she nodded compliantly. "It would be good," she said, "if the only people who were allowed to ask that question had themselves come from another place and were still getting used to it here. That would be alright—like patients in a line for the dentist discussing their teeth." Again the old man put her right: "You see, you don't know this yet—but here no one speaks to each other in a medical waiting room, and if they do they only talk about the weather. But mostly they're silent, that's just the way it is. Although they greet you to begin with, of course."

Fifty-year-old M had very quickly adopted the persona of a blushing ingenue in this conversation. She always slipped very easily into this role, as if she was permanently unsure of her age and position, and she hardly even noticed the man was speaking to her as if she were a child. "So where are you from?" he asked again, as if her first answer had gone astray and he was kindly giving her another try. M, suddenly deciding she would say and do only as she wanted, told him the truth: "The capital. I've just arrived." The whiskery old man nodded. "But where were you born?" The conversation began to resemble that game in which someone sticks a piece of paper to your forehead with the name of a literary hero or a historic villain and you have to ask cunning questions in order to work out who you are. But she never found out where all this was leading, because at that very moment her phone began to ring, summoning her with its piercing tone, and the old man shrugged and retreated back to his seat in the corner. "Yes!" M shouted into the phone, "I'm here and I'm not sure what to do ..."

The organizers of the festival in the neighboring country hadn't forgotten about her at all, they were still waiting for her, and the event, planned for that evening, was going ahead. They suggested she should take a train, a slow suburban one, stopping at every little station, and make her way to the town of F on the border, where a taxi would be waiting for her. "Can you buy a ticket?" The voice on the other end of the line was anxious, confirming once again her new status as a child or a crazy person, someone at any rate who couldn't be trusted to look after themselves and needed special and careful attention. M assured them that she could manage. The train was due to leave in forty minutes.

Now that everything was settled and her travel plans had been sorted out, she thought with regret of the possibilities that had been glinting seductively in the air around her and had now vanished. The plotline with the stolen suitcase and police reports was perhaps a little over-the-top, and yet the despair and confusion that it had promised had seemed attractive to her somehow. She felt a vague sense of yearning at the thought that she could get a cheap hotel room in this town in which she suddenly found herself, and just lie down on the made bed without even taking off her shoes, like her fellow traveler from the train. Four walls enclosing an anonymous cube of air, a narrow mirror, a coffee machine if she was lucky, and, apart from her passport, which she would have to show to check in, nothing else would be demanded of her, she would be of no interest to anyone. And then, she thought with a slight chuckle, she could even get to that museum.

6.

To the museum, she murmured as she retraced her steps with exaggerated cheerfulness: the pedestrian crossing, the beer bar, the square in front of the station with its parked cars, the pigeon by the rubbish bin, the people on the platform and on the train, a double-decker with big windows, exactly like the one that had stood at this platform a few hours ago, or perhaps it was the very same train. There were already a lot of people crowded on the platform. *Nowhere for an apple to fall*, as one might say in her own language, a flexing, twisting, nearly all-powerful language, and one that she now mistrusted, because who knew what was being said in this language right now by her compatriots, sent to fight in a neighboring country. Who, and how, were they killing as they spoke it? She was still convinced that the beast was to blame, and people had merely spent too long in the atmosphere of its poisoned breath and had come to resemble it. They had been brutalized, in short. But it was harder when it came to the language, which was far older than the beast: a layer of horrid slime covered it, erupting in rotting pustules, violent new words had appeared in it, like *collateral, slotted, double tap.* It was as if the language had gone wild, had stopped recognizing its own. M herself hardly wanted to go near it, she was still biding her time.

There was more space on the upper deck and she found a seat by a window. At last, the train started moving and a group of teenagers in boy scout uniforms, with stout boots, who had occupied the steps at the end of the carriage, were already playing a game she didn't recognize, laying out illustrated glossy cards in a complicated pattern. The passengers who were still walking up and down the train had to step over the cards, but no one seemed bothered by this and some passengers even exchanged a few words of encouragement with the players. M stretched out her legs, closed her eyes, and tried to doze, but she couldn't. She was wide awake, thinking, back in the twilit tunnel she knew so well, and where she tried not to spend too much time. Her head at such moments seemed to be in flight, or in freefall, as if the ground had suddenly disappeared from under her feet, and it wasn't clear whether or when it would reappear. M opened her eyes and firmly pressed her heels onto the floor just in case.

The constant sensation of falling (as if you were weightless, transparent, or as if the people and objects around you were, and you were falling through them, down and down, smiling and apologizing all the while as you sank) was now natural, even if she wasn't yet used to it, and it was an effort to recall a time when things had been different. Perhaps she should have attempted to stop this feeling of falling, to "ground herself," as was sometimes said, but it was hard to believe this was possible; after all, where was this ground supposed to be? "She's completely lost control over her biography," M's lover had once said of another woman, and M had grinned in response, as if to acknowledge the fact that one needed to keep a tight hold of one's biography, not let it wriggle away and run amok.

As we already know, there was a lake in the place where M now lived, and on a bridge over the lake, some large stone humanimals lay back-to-back. Two things are known for certain about sphinxes: they spend their whole lives solving all possible kinds of riddles in their heads, and if you aren't able to help them with this, then their animal natures overcome them and they eat you alive, like a cat eats a mouse. But when M looked into their wonderful stone faces, turned towards her with expressions of grief-filled dignity, even tenderness (although God knows who these tender feelings were for) it was impossible to suspect them of any such harm. Their hair was braided with ribbons, their breasts were bare—in fact the breasts of one were ringed with waterproof paint, white around the left nipple, blue around the right nipple. These stony beasts did not try to conceal their animal nature, their tails were bare, sinewy, with a tuft at the end, and their arms were covered in unpleasant rough fur from the wrists up. The dog M had imagined earlier would doubtless have barked at the sphinxes, recognizing them, with their dual nature, as capable of anything, despite their apparent serenity. But perhaps that was why M didn't have a dog: she herself was no longer certain that she belonged to only one species: her words, her thoughts, even her deeds, might expose her own monstrous nature at any moment. After all, she thought, despite the years she'd spent filled with hatred and revulsion for the beast, she had lived with it for as long as she could remember, in the same cage, or maybe even in its belly like Jonah inside the whale, and she hardly remembered a time when the beast wasn't with her. Could this mean that she was its offspring, a smaller clone—one of the millions who seem outwardly sad and gentle, but are just waiting for the moment to pounce with claws outstretched and eat anyone who doesn't reciprocate their feelings? This thought took such a hold in M that she sometimes caught herself reaching towards the mirror to check whether red fur hadn't begun growing over her own forearms.

The train proceeded slowly, as if in a dream, stopping at every tiny station, and at each stop more people got off than on. Along the quiet platforms, shrubs flowered with a furious energy; they looked a little like elderflower, but in place of the white blossom a profusion of crimson foamed darkly down the green foliage. almost to the ground. Ancient safety signs urged caution; they looked as if they hadn't been replaced since the seventies, when M herself had been a child, gazing out at just such signs on platforms with their once-bright paint and the picture of a person falling backwards onto the railway line in front of a train. And then M saw that very same image (or one nearly identical) and for a moment it seemed as if this involved dream was coming to an end: she was on a train to the dacha, the years falling away from her as she traveled, she was ten years old again, now she was eight and now five—and she was long expected.

She realized now why she had been so repelled by the thought of a museum visit. Many years before she had read a story in which a sudden summer storm forced a traveler into a provincial museum filled with sculptures and a dreary fossil collection. But the museum turned out to be a trap: there was no end to the halls and rooms, they multiplied, increasing like mutating matter, and it was quite impossible to reach even the end of the wing. Above the traveler sprouted more and more floors of rooms with rustling curtains, the carcasses of grand pianos and mile after mile of oil paintings; alongside these were what we now call "installation art": landscapes with lifeless ponds and confected fog. All around him swarmed crowds of people, just as in the afterlife where everyone meets again—in fact this could well have been the afterlife. I don't remember how the traveler escaped out of the building to where it was deserted, cold, where the snow lay half-melted in the blackened, blistered earth and it smelt of dank water. The streetlamps were different here, but also deeply familiar. The traveler had tumbled down a rabbit hole and been thrown out into the forbidden place, his own home country—but not the place of his memories, the actual, genuine place, with its executions and political slogans, where he could be devoured without a second thought. And, thought M, this might happen to anyone who wanted to go back to *that* home, throwing off memory like a heavy unwanted burden; returning to the warm womb, the dacha with its apple-patterned curtains. No, better to go on to the town of F, and from there to somewhere else.

Out of the corner of her eye M could see an elderly couple in a row of seats ahead of her. They were talking together quietly, rustling something the woman had unrolled to show the man. Two guidebooks and a map already lay on the folded-out table and the couple kept bending over them, seemingly to check their route. For the first time, M wondered where exactly she was going. The name of the town of F meant nothing to her, she was in these parts for the very first time.

She rummaged in her bag for her phone. The internet guessed what was on the novelist's mind—as soon as she started typing the first letter it offered her a wealth of information about the town and its attractions. It was on the coast, at the border with the neighboring country, and there were apparently "things to do in F": a pedestrianized main street, the obligatory local museum (this one called the Phantomoteke for some reason), beaches, restaurants, hotels with names like "Paradise" and "La Vie sur l'Eau." One of the hotels particularly interested her as it bore the name "Grand Hotel Petukh," which, for anyone who spoke her native language, was an amusing choice. This is where she would have stayed, said M to herself, had she not been merely passing through. She'd have unpacked her bag with a semblance of purpose, put three books in a pile on the bedside table, and gone to inspect the sea view. That this would never come to pass, caused in her a sudden wave of annoyance: the accident which had brought her here was merely a very unexceptional fold in life's fabric, without meaning or consequence.

The couple sitting ahead of her continued leafing through tourist maps. Then the man stood and made his way to the end of the carriage, using a thin stick, not to lean on, but to make broad sweeps in front of him, knocking the tip against the backs of chairs and over the floor. In this manner M learned that the man was blind.

At every small stop a few more passengers left the train and were usually met from the platform. It reminded M a little of the parents waiting outside the theatre after a children's show in her childhood, how they would stand in a crowd, attempting to catch each child as they came out until every last one was gone. It was a Friday evening train, everyone was going home for the weekend: young soldiers on leave, students from the city, tired office workers. The little stations were now deep in the countryside, the roads lay motionless under the late sun, and it was as if the whole population of each village had gathered on the platforms to wait for their loved ones; in one place someone was even holding balloons. M could of course have alighted from the train at any of these stops, but she couldn't begin to imagine what she would do there, or where she would spend the night. A tall girl in a leather jacket bent to embrace her diminutive mother. A sign on a ticket office read: "Closed."

7.

M's cell phone was getting low on battery even though she'd topped it up in the town of G. She began feeling around in her bag for the charger, but there was nowhere to plug it in anyway. She couldn't find it, it wasn't in the bag—the novelist had clearly left it in the Turkish café although she remembered telling herself not to forget it. The little yellow pillar on the screen indicating how much battery she had left was very low—twenty percent or so, just enough to get to the taxi. The train was at last rolling into F, its final stop, and everyone began getting to their feet.

There were enough of them left in the train to form an unbroken stream, flooding the platform and pulling her along with it. She noted in passing a uniformed policeman, surrounded by a group of people standing with lowered heads who were clearly not locals. They were speaking, and M supposed that the policeman must have asked them the question that so irritated her: where are you from? She felt sympathy with them, yet kept up with the crowd, hardly slowing her step. She vaguely recognized one of the backs ahead of her, as if from a former life. Oh, yes: it was the man with the ponytail and hair clips. His head was higher than the others, the fair hair gathered with such perfect neatness, as if he hadn't been traveling all day like her, changing from one train to the next. He suddenly turned and glanced at her, and then quickly looked away as though the sight had been unexpected and unpleasant.

M felt embarrassed, as if she'd been caught doing something wrong, especially as she knew the hair clips and the chin had been recorded, had already installed themselves in her memory. It sometimes happened like that: you could be captivated by a stranger's appearance, not by its perfection, but by the combination of its imperfections—and then the position of the head or the sight of a narrow ankle covered in pale freckles could become wedged in the mind like a splinter in the flesh. The sensation, so very familiar to her, could hardly be called desire; she had absolutely no wish to find herself in a hotel room on her own with this man, and yet she wanted to continue looking at him, as you might at a deer, or a rabbit huddling in the low grass and gazing back at you with its huge eye. But, with people, staring became a form of touch, and it was shameful to be caught in the act and have your gaze pondered and analyzed. She had read somewhere that in prehistoric times, in the dark ancestral chaos when the sense of sight was only emerging, it was the prerogative of the predator. That predatory eye, still not quite formed, registered the movement of other bodies and discerned the outline of food running away so it could hasten in pursuit and snatch up the alluring object to swallow it whole. Her interest in stranger's ankles, it seemed, was another thing linking her with the beast, she too wished to run after them—although she had no desire to snap at them or gobble them up; her little internal beast was to all intents and purposes a herbivore, save these occasional inappropriate acts.

Once in a forest in autumn M had watched a dog (a city dog, unused to rural life) trap a shrew, pressing it to the ground with its paw so the shrew couldn't move. The dog performed this with ease and cunning, but was then thrown into sudden confusion, almost desperation, and began squealing and barking to summon its owner: it had no idea what to do with the shrew next, and was even pleased to be dragged away from its prey. M suspected that something like this could happen to her in the same situation.

She loved street photography: unknown people pulled out of their hidden lives and transposed onto paper so they could be gazed at without hindrance. But these were only images, resemblances. She'd read of a French artist who made an art of stalking, so to speak, passersby, following them, unnoticed, along the streets of Paris, and gathering a sort of dossier on some of them—and all of this without any interest in love, just a simple desire to see what would happen next. M herself could happily follow a pair of plum-colored ballet pumps or a head of tousled red hair wherever they might lead, and it could easily end in catastrophe, with the loss of both phone and suitcase, and then complete oblivion, as in that little Swiss book. Equally, the person you were following might suddenly stop, turn around and ask in a furious voice what you thought you were doing and how you dared dog their footsteps. The thought of this happening made M freeze in shame.

It also happened, and not infrequently, that she would be on her way somewhere when she noticed a stranger, someone she had no interest in, had been walking ahead of her for a long time, turning the same corners and clearly taking the same route as her. When she realized this, she felt such a weight on her, as if she really had been following the person all that time and surely they must have noticed and any moment now would turn full face and demand an explanation. Indeed the sense of personal shame she seemed to have been born with excluded all possibility of carelessness and frivolity from her life, making her behavior quite safe for all those around her; it had always been so, here, in this country, no less than in the country of her birth.

The crowd flowed on, its course bending around a florist's stall with sunflowers, and a little kiosk selling pretzels, until it spilled onto the square outside, where everyone hastened away in a counterclockwise direction, soon disappearing around a corner, including the man with the hair clips. M remained, washed up like a piece of driftwood, by the taxi stand. She had assumed that someone would be waiting for her with a sign, like at an airport, and now she didn't quite know what to do. There weren't many taxis, four yellow ones and a foreign car of a different make and design. This had to be the car sent by the festival. The driver sat indifferent to the world, his hands folded on the wheel, as if he had no business being there. But the novelist was determined to get to her destination, and she flung back the taxi door, saying her name, and the driver gave an amiable nod.

"So where are we heading then?" he asked after they'd turned into the street, quite as if he didn't know. "I thought you had all the details," replied M brightly. "They're expecting me in the city of O at a festival. I have a performance tonight at 8 p.m." "It's a good way," said the driver. "We'll try to get you there on time."

The town was already behind them, the bus stops were few and far between. They passed some melancholy warehouses and a well-trodden space where a traveling circus with off-white tents had set up camp, a cluster of wagons with two windows, and a disproportionately large banner: PETER COHN'S CIRCUS. She watched two workers spraying the tarpaulin with a heavy-duty hose, washing off the day's dust. Evening was approaching, and presumably a show, but it was otherwise quiet all around; Serpent Woman and the trapeze artists must have been ensconced in their wagons.

A little further on was the turning onto the main road and beyond it the border. "You can get a coffee here," said the driver, nodding at a gas station. "You must be tired from the journey." For some reason the novelist seized upon this opportunity, as if she couldn't bear to part with the town of F. They bought coffee and sat at wooden benches outside. M told the story of the disappearing train and they both nodded, recalling the days when there was a part of each carriage reserved for smokers and timetables had some bearing on reality. In turn the taxi driver told her he'd had Covid four times now, that the virus was the product of a secret and sinister global organization tasked with killing off old people because they were living too long and costing governments too much. M didn't even try to contradict him—clearly by now they had the sort of solidarity that arises between those who have begun a long journey together and know there is still a long way ahead. There was a pause—the sort that usually preceded the question about where she had come from, but the taxi driver avoided this topic and asked instead where she was to be delivered in the city of O.

M had no idea and admitted it freely. "Perhaps you could call them while we're sitting here and ask? My phone has nearly lost its charge or I could have checked the address . . . but I thought they must have given you that information?" "Ring who?" asked the driver, shaking his braids in confusion. They drove back to the railway station, the novelist all the while gesticulating and sighing and apologizing profusely for the silly mix-up.

By now there were as many foreign taxis as there were local ones, but no one waiting for M. She walked along the pavement, bending and glancing into each car and then stepping back to get out her phone. Her new acquaintance had already taken on passengers but before he left he waved at her from the driver's seat and lifted his hands to the sky to indicate that the world had gone mad and one should hardly be surprised at such unpleasant twists of fate.

8.

Another train must have arrived because a lively crowd began streaming out of the station building, which was hidden under scaffolding, all looking as if they knew where they were going. The long notes of the dial tone sounded on the phone M now held out before her at the midpoint between ear and eye. No one was picking up. It was as if they had decided they would get on fine without her, but had forgotten to let her know. M walked back and forth for a little while longer, and then, without knowing why, she joined the crowd at the back, still holding out her phone. Together with them, as if on a joyous march, she walked down the wide street, with its shops and cheerful café tables, the crowd gradually melting into groups and scattering in different directions. M slowed and checked her phone. The screen was dark, the phone quite dead. Now no one could give her the instructions she needed.

Letting herself move with the flow of people, M walked on up the street, past the park and the shop signs, glancing at fast food restaurants and other people's plates on tables under canvas café awnings. She was now cut off, a spare limb, a nonexistent existence; no one knew where she was or what had happened to her, and no one could demand anything of her or call her to heel. Those duties and promises, which only an hour ago had appeared so immutable, no longer had any power over her, and yet she'd played no active part in this transformation. The novelist walked on, slightly embarrassed by the unceasing rumble of her suitcase, which didn't seem to mind where it was being dragged to. She noticed as she walked that her inner self had stopped wheeling and fluttering, banging itself against the walls in search of an exit, and had gradually quietened, becoming soft, childlike, even poking out curious snail horns to see what would happen next.

A hotel appeared in front of her, as if it had sprung up out of nowhere—like in a dream where you don't understand how you moved from a ship's deck, for example, to a school classroom; the cabinet shelves lined with glass jars of natural specimens, among them a pickled rat with a hopeless, crooked snarl, resembling your old history teacher.

The hotel was basic, one of those chains where they take pride in making the traveler forget she has traveled a long way and is now in a very different place—wherever you are, you are greeted by the sight of the same oatmeal-colored divan, the same turquoise boiled sweets in a deep vase, and in the rooms always the same short pile carpet and combined shower gel and shampoo in one dispenser. M entered the building as if born to flit along its winding corridors like a shade, and make the obliging coffee machine honk and splutter its dark potion. She was hardly aware of checking in or even how she paid, so desperately did she want to find herself in her room, to fall backwards onto the bed and feel as if she had at last arrived. But she did manage to ask at reception if they had a charger she could use—and wasn't in the least surprised when they told her that other guests had taken all the chargers, and there was no way to obtain one. The day's events were progressing exactly as if preordained, and the telephone, silent as a root of wormwood, was itself clearly one of the necessary conditions for this.

From the wide bed where she lay she could see that it was still completely light outside, and this too was unsurprising: it was not meant to get dark, the day would stretch on, extending like a telescope, an empty vessel that could be filled as desired; although she herself had no desires, neither the clearly understood sort nor those that manifest as a vague scent or faint rustle. When she turned her head away from the window and to the left she could see the hotel artwork on the walls, undemanding but lent an air of respectability by the frames: over the rickety little table there was a still life of waxen lilies in a round bubble of water and glass; and on the nearer wall a pair of playful dolphins with snouts like ducks' bills. Not long before, M had heard something about dolphins which had caught her attention and she'd promised herself that she'd check if it was true and find out more, but once again she'd not had the energy. She'd learned that dolphins were basically dogs—that is, hardly differing from the creatures we have as our daily companions—except in one aspect, the result of a crucial decision they'd once made. It seemed that, among the prehistoric creatures that crawled out of the deep, there were those that changed their minds, and after a time on land with us, swapping gills for lungs and learning to breathe the heavy air of the atmosphere, they'd decided to go home, back to the watery depths. So it seemed that, too, was a possibility—and even for M, who was certain that there could never be any going back home, this example of double transformation, into one animal and then another, which bore no resemblance to the original, was almost consoling. It meant you could belong to both worlds at once, leaping up and hanging between water and air, oblivious of who you once were. Oblivion was quite impossible in M's case, but the thought that there were creatures who had successfully changed their nature so radically was vaguely encouraging.

She was hungry but didn't want to get up. Lying like this, on the made bed, was part of the whole ritual for arriving in a hotel room, along with the two pairs of shoes placed side by side, noses to the wall; the white shirts hanging on little wire shoulders in the closed wardrobe; and the three books piled on the far bedside table, as if she planned to stay a long time, reading herself to sleep each night. You could even go so far as to say that the room M was in resembled the drawer in someone else's bedside table, everything neatly arranged, the organization of objects reflecting their function, and nothing spoiling the overall harmony: no crooked corner or unforeseen hole to cause a pang of distress. But outside the little piece of furniture everything was made of such yawning holes and gaps, the terrible wrenching of matter, of horror and trembling, shame and guilt, death and destruction. Death and destruction, she repeated silently to herself; over which she had not the slightest power. Still, here, in this tightly shut cupboard drawer, she had been given a moment's respite, and she intended to use it, whatever happened.

She lay like that for a good while, then rose with one sudden movement, astonished that her relaxed body still obeyed her, and went down to reception to get a street map of F, leaving her cell phone lying in her room like an umbrella when no rain is forecast.

All she could bring to mind of what she'd read of the myriad wonders of F was the Grand Hotel Petukh and the museum, although the museum's name swam up strangely warped in her memory: *Phantorama*, was it? *Phantomat*? A visit to the museum was by this hour out of the question and she didn't need a hotel; she already had a plastic key card to remind her every time she put her hand in her pocket that she had a roof over her head.

Outside, in the fresh air, she made a beeline for the nearest fast-food stand, drawn by the smell of grilled meat, and a few moments later she stood on the pavement holding a weighty paper parcel in both hands, the wrapper darkening with grease. The novelist, trembling with newly awoken hunger, began eating from it: morsels of animal flesh, salted gherkin, wilted lettuce leaves, working her way down through the parcel's contents until only the damp paper was left.

Here she should have gone straight back to the hotel, into her drawer, under her cloak, and closed her eyes at last, but some relic of ancient instinct (the memory of dry land, perhaps) demanded that she take the actions appropriate to her arrival in an unknown town. Quite what these were she wasn't yet sure, so she wandered towards the town center, looking about her and sniffing the air, as if she was being dragged along on a leash.

The Grand Hotel Petukh was suddenly before her without her making any particular effort to seek it out; as if there was no avoiding it, as if all her journeys had been leading to it. It was a fancy-looking hotel with a rich chocolate-brown façade, the windows outlined in crimson, like eyes lined in kohl pencil. M wandered in under its wing, hardly knowing herself what she was searching for and whether she really wanted to find it, sensing immediately that there was nothing there for her. The lobby was cool and smart; the bar offered a wide selection of drinks in golden and cranberry hues; the grand staircase seemed to be in the process of unfurling itself; and the walls were lined with ancestral portraits, surveying her with expressions of barely restrained hostility, despite her having nothing to say to them today. But now she was there she made the most of it, ordering a glass of white wine and sitting down at a table outside, her legs stretched in front of her, gazing at the passing crowds.

Petukh, in the country she came from, was a name for those who were in prison or "in the zone," and, within that prison system, had been made into the lowest of the low, the untouchables. Everything about this phrase required explanation or translation for anyone who lived outside that country and yet wanted to understand what it meant. The "zones" were vast areas of prison camps, where both criminals and those who weren't guilty of any crime, but had been convicted for acts that didn't accord to the spirit of the state, were imprisoned together. The zones and the people living in them were huge in number and extent: *no indemnity from jail or poverty*, as the well-known proverb in her language went, meaning that it was a fate that could befall anyone, someone standing holding a blank piece of paper in a lonely protest, for example. After all, anything can be read into a blank piece of paper—from a call to civic disobedience, say, to the overthrow of the whole state.

M had heard it said that far more people in her country had been in prison than had a passport and with it the chance to leave the country and see other places and how others lived. And "in the zone," where they abided by thousands of unwritten rules, there was a caste of untouchables: the humiliated ones, the *petukh*. To make a person into one of these untouchables was to physically force him down to the bottom of the heap, to the lowest depths, where touch or even conversation was impossible. There was what you could call a special ritual for the purpose: either the unlucky victim was collectively raped, thus designating him common prey and his body common property, so anyone henceforth could use him as and when they wanted; or the prisoner's head was dunked in a bucket of human waste, face first, profaning the victim, as if the waste of the collective body could never now be washed from him. Anyone could become a *petukh*; it was enough just to displease those who ruled the camp, the so-called *vory*, or thieves, or to break one of the strange prohibitions making up the thieves' code, which was more important and more terrifying than any civil law. One of the rules was this: if you touched or made contact with a *petukh* you too were deemed unclean, as if the virus could transfer from one body to another, and you would automatically come under suspicion and could easily become one of the untouchables yourself, a nonhuman: something other.

The wine had a salty metallic tang as if it had been poured from a tin flask and what one might have called the bouquet (a faint distant shadow of fruit or honey) was altogether absent. Salt and cold had filled M's mouth, leaving no space for anything else, and united they reigned.

9.

The pack of cigarettes she held was long and narrow like a coffin. The blue lid folded back completely, and on it, of course, the standard picture in muted dreary tones: a nurse, or morgue worker, covering the face of a young corpse with a white sheet; an example of what smoking leads to. The novelist M loved to promise herself that she would one day write an essay about these images, which accompanied her everywhere now. They made her so agitated that in kiosks sometimes she asked for the same cigarettes, but with a different warning image on the packet, perhaps the one with the tracksuited youth lying morosely on a bedspread and the caption explaining that smoking causes impotence. Sometimes she got the anguished faces of babies (symbolizing infertility) or grieving orphaned families (symbolizing the obvious). They were still better than the close-up pictures of damaged internal organs, blackened fingers or bleeding ulcers, also plentiful. The latter were more literal and immediate in their effect—their effectiveness evident by the efforts M made to avoid them and to choose images of outcomes that were no less real but were (how to put it?) somewhat more oblique.

In the world M now inhabited these unpleasant images on cigarette packets were the only reminders of disease and death and what both wrought upon the human body. They were blunt and ugly, laying bare a frightening side of life. Medical leaflets and ads in women's magazines had the same warnings, of course, and yet these images were more delicate, hopeful even—only the letters of the text in small print were allowed to touch upon the fearful and repugnant reality, but the pictures themselves were of beautiful melancholic women or distinguished-looking old men who hadn't lost their dignity or their mind as they approached the grave. The horror and pain of existence was now only evident on boxes of Marlboro, Lucky Strike and so on, as if their consumers were by default so far from the civilized world that there was no need to hide its hideous underbelly from them—in fact that underside was all they were allowed to see, as a foretelling of inevitable retribution for the disregard they had shown their own lives. It was all vaguely reminiscent of old frescoes in churches depicting the bodies and souls of sinners subjected to all sorts of highly refined torments, and viewed without sympathy by decent Christians, unless of course they too were concealing guilt. In the new secular world the process had been rationalized: the miserable prognosis was transmitted directly to the sinners and to them alone. After all, who else would be studying the images on cigarette packets? Now M at last drew a cigarette out of its little coffin and began rolling it between her fingers, as if in expectation.

It was a Friday in summer, and the proximity of the coast could be felt somehow: that indefinable tautness of sea air, perhaps. M sat in a dreamy stupor. No one in the world, or at least no one in F, had any idea who she was or what sins lay on her soul; she was determined to make the opportunity that had fallen to her last as long as possible. She was beyond the reach of those who might be concerned by her fate, alarmed or even annoyed at her sudden disappearance into thin air; even she had no particular desire to ask questions of herself; all she felt now was a sleepy sense of affection. For the first time in she didn't know how long, she forgot where she was from and why it was important, and she even barely thought about the beast, as if she wasn't herself but someone else, someone quite other. In her childhood it was only on high days and holidays, New Year's Eve or Mayday, that they spread a starched tablecloth over the table, and, on ordinary days, days that didn't merit such an honor, the table was covered with a patterned oilcloth, and nobody minded if you left spots of jam or spilled soup on it. Over time its shiny surface became pitted with scars and rips that were interesting to look at and idly poke your fingers through as you sat and dreamed. Tiny crumbs sometimes got caught in the rips and then stayed there forever, becoming brittle and gravelly in their little nooks, safe from cleaning; except during a spring clean when everything was shaken out and washed and the crumbs, too, disappeared—but that was only after a long time.

A fine rain began to fall, and stopped almost immediately, but M didn't move.

Although she was enjoying the sense of peace she at last felt, watching people passing this way and that on the summer evening, with the relaxed strolling pace only ever used at the seaside; and at the children clutching ice cream cones, the adults talking over their heads, she had the vague sense of something gnawing at her, something that had direct relevance to her, and finally she remembered what it was. It was an old story, and many years ago it had left such an impression on her that she had never once returned to it, so firmly ensconced in her mind was its moral.

The story concerned the travels of a linguist, a specialist in dialects and varieties of Arabic, who journeys with hopeful excitement to the edge of the desert, to stay a week in a place he'd visited some years before and remembered fondly. It began with the man's nose, very literally, a description of the professor smelling the exotic scents that had once given him so much pleasure: smoke from the grilling meat, dung, the wind blowing in from the vast endlessness, the fruit rotting in the heat. But then the focus shifted to the linguist's tongue, as one might expect. The friendly café owner had died or disappeared, and another had taken his place, a gruff unpleasant man who refuses to talk to the professor in Arabic, the language he knows so well, and instead mutters at him in broken French. At this point the learned professor should have returned to the comforts of the Grand Hotel

Saharien to nurse his disappointment, but he cannot be dissuaded from his long-held plan of purchasing even a single souvenir, an example of the local craft he so prizes. So the unknown man reluctantly escorts him through the wastes and backyards to a nomadic settlement where he might purchase some rare item made from camel's udder, a collector's trophy, and leaves him to his fate. The desert people, who have no idea who the professor is, or how delighted he would be to talk to them in their own dialect, waste no time: before he can open his mouth they truss him like a sheep and skillfully cut out his tongue at its very root. The very next day they strike camp and an unimaginably different life begins for the professor.

Now his task is to entertain his new owners, to dance, grunting, like a bear on a chain, throwing himself with a terrifying roar at the women of the tribe, giving them no little delight. He lives in a fog of pain and amnesia, oblivious of who he is and where he came from. He becomes more and more skilled in his new art and comes to be seen as a very favorable acquisition, a chattel that can be sold on. Many miles and many encampments later this is exactly what happens: in a house surrounded by high walls in a desert settlement he is passed on to a venerable buyer. But then something goes wrong, a half-forgotten language is blown into the internal courtyard as if by the wind, and the *petukh* refuses to dance or grunt any longer, hardly knowing why himself. A bloody episode follows, the details of which M had long forgotten, but she distinctly remembered what came next: the once-renowned linguist wanders out of the house where he is imprisoned and no one stops him. He finds himself on a half-empty street at dusk where an indifferent observer watches him hopping and cavorting, his figure gradually growing smaller as he disappears back into the desert, further and further away from what had once been, and had now ceased to be, his world.

It's hard to say how the story of the linguist related to the novelist M's current situation. She had never been able to move between one mode of speech and another, like an artful mockingbird. And, as we know, for a while now she had been a novelist in name only; either language had stopped obeying her or she had stopped being able to command it. This wasn't because she had hardened towards her native tongue—it was innocent and so defenseless that anyone could hang their horrid bells on it and make it caper about imitating a beast. After all, as M knew, this wasn't the first time something like this had happened to her language, and not just to hers, the flesh and skin of other languages wore the marks of their treatment at the hands of former masters: bruises, notches, embedded jags of metal. No, it was pointless shaming language, and it was unjust, too. Better to settle scores with oneself, although in truth M hadn't really done that either: the bill had come without her having asked for it, as it had for that woman who received a scarf every single night identical to the one she had used to stifle her baby many years before, and the persistent nature of the gift made it clear that she was already living in hell. M had never had anything in common with the beast—at least, that is what she'd always thought. But the beast had expanded in dimension and now consisted of everyone who had ever lived in the land where she was born (and where not so long ago she had gone to bed each night and woken up each morning) and also of those who spoke and wrote in the language she called her own—so it did seem that she must be the beast after all. That is, she was herself, of course, but the beast as well, the beast and then herself and then the beast, and sometimes she noticed in the face or in the shoulders of the person she was speaking to something like a spasm, which told her that it was the beast they saw in her, the beast first and foremost.

There was nothing that could be done to change this, not even, it seemed, by those people, far better than her, who looked so small from a distance but had bravely gone out to face the beast barehanded. It defied all understanding that the beast, after eating them, only got bigger and stronger; or how their courage inspired and emboldened others, right up to the moment when its jaws crunched down on them, and they became part of the whole organism, an edifying example, a live-action *nature morte*, a convincing argument for hopelessness. It seemed as if the only way to get rid of the beast was to get rid of oneself; or to remain silent forever to avoid inadvertently speaking in the voice of the beast. In theory M might have found a way to argue against this oversimplification, but her hands, her body, not to mention her tongue, were still—as if they too agreed that silence was best.

But today, today

10.

but today M found herself by pure chance outside her own predestined arc of travel—like the forgotten avocado sandwich on the train that might still be traveling on its journey, or else might have met a suitable mouth. Something small, pink and featherlight was drifting across the asphalt in the breeze—cherry blossoms, but not real ones; fake, paper flowers from a packet, lying on the ground nearby. It wasn't that the novelist felt herself to be suddenly and unexpectedly different, but that a part of her was anaesthetized or had simply vanished. It was as if a weight had been lifted from her; as if her head, perhaps, or just the top of it, had been removed, giving her a chilly, tender sensation. So it should come as no surprise that she now behaved in a way that was not at all characteristic, as if she wasn't herself but someone quite different—and this is what happened: among the throng of unknown and almost indistinguishable people, appeared a back that at first looked oddly familiar, then more and more recognizable, and all at once M left her seat and, without even knowing why, she followed the back, in exactly the same manner as that French artist, unburdened by guilt, shame, awkwardness, uncertainty, and all other such baggage.

The man with the hair clips (all perfectly placed and even glittering slightly in the sunlight, keeping the blonde hair neatly confined) was striding on his way. He looked like an athlete: a high jumper, or a tennis player who had just finished training, had showered and was now walking along with the same precision of movement as when he volleyed a ball at the net. M kept a sensible distance from him, but the street led them both like a river, with its whirlpools and eddies, past crossroads and bookshop windows, and the distance between them kept extending or getting shorter. Like a proper spy, M would slow down or cross the road or stop to light a cigarette, trying to stay unobserved and finding the slightly seedy game more and more pleasurable.

If she had stopped to think and consider her actions, she surely would have realized how dubious it all was, and might even have asked herself: why this person? What did she want from him, apart from the opportunity to gaze at his shoulder blades and wrists? How on earth would she justify it all to herself? But she was so preoccupied with the effort of simply keeping up without being noticed that she had no time for such thoughts, or for any thoughts at all, in fact. Still, she did notice that he had indeed taken a shower and changed into an identical fresh T-shirt, and that he took long steps, although she had no idea where he was going. The town was imperceptibly coming to an end, the object of her attention had not headed towards the seaside promenade, as she might have expected, but in a completely different direction. The shop windows and cafés had long been left behind, and now they were walking along empty streets with parked cars, and balconies with parasols and window boxes. Then these, too, ended and they were on the edge of town, right at its neglected fringe, where the only possible way forward was across empty land. A gas station flashed at an intersection, beyond it some storage buildings and metal garages. M slowed her pace as much as she could and hung back, hardly daring to ask herself how much longer this would go on, and what would happen next. There was no one around besides her and the man with the hair clips—they were a tiny procession of two. Ahead of them on a green hill shone the white buildings of a hospital or a hotel, and closer, to the right, set back a little from the road, were the dusty tents, wagons, trailers and the banner with PETER COHN'S CIRCUS written on it. She'd gone a very long way it seemed, and, not for the first time on this strange day, she was back where she'd already been, like a piece in a game of chess, briefly held and rolled in the hand before being set back down in the same square.

And now it came to pass, just as she had imagined it: the object of her attention, who had been walking all this time, and paying no heed to what lay around him and behind him, suddenly stopped, turned to face M, and moved towards her with such indignant fury that he covered the fifty meters between them in seconds.

He was even taller than she'd thought, his pale eyes were unpleasant, and she felt as if he'd caught her putting a hand in his pocket, had seized her by the wrist and wasn't about to let go. He even bent towards her slightly, as if to intimidate her, and at that her bold and frivolous mood entirely deserted her. *Oh god what have I done?* groaned a voice in her head, and simultaneously she heard the man asking a similar question, the entirely predictable: "What do you want? Why are you following me?"

11.

The novelist stepped back. Her inner self trembled and murmured like a bush in the wind, but her outer self behaved with unexpected presence of mind. She drew herself up with dignity, answering with feeling, and in English, that she wasn't sure quite what he meant, and that, if he really wanted to know, she was on her way to Peter Cohn's Circus, and nodded her head in the direction of the wagons and tents. His pale eyes studied her for a while longer, then the man with the hair clips replied curtly: "OK, my apologies." He turned and went on his way, only once or twice turning to glance back suspiciously.

There was nothing else to be done, she was forced now to turn into the circus grounds, which were empty and deserted, although many bright posters advertised the evening's show. M could hardly remember when she'd last been to the circus. The thought of trained animals heaving from one drum to another, or poking their muzzles at cards covered in numbers they cannot comprehend, made her cringe in misery. The clowns weren't funny, they were oddly terrifying, and only the spangled acrobat turning slowly counterclockwise under the dome of the tent made her feel anything remotely like respectful solidarity. In childhood, of course, it had all been different, but what remained in her memory was not the circus itself but an old film about the circus in which the foreign tap dancing star was fired from a cannon straight up at the moon before pulling a short black wig from her head and smiling at the audience, shaking out her homely flaxen tresses.

The film was made in the midthirties, a period of arrests, executions, prison camps. And yet the film itself ended with a scene of utter wonder: a huge airy construction, shining white and tiered like a wedding cake, billowed upwards from the center of the circus ring. On each layer young citizens in gym pants moved their arms and legs in synchrony. This collective swaying motion was a celebration of the new life and its new delights, although without the small print of the cigarette packet. Somewhere in the locked home M had left behind there was a photograph she had inherited of an unknown person, perhaps a distant relative, lying in a hammock, her head thrown back, her pretty, plump arms outstretched. On the back of the photo were the words "Summer 1938" (the summer of 1938 was the height of the Terror) and nothing more. Did the young woman know what was going on around her? Did she know about the breaking of bones and the pooling of bloody matter? And who could say how the year had ended for her? After all, the beast had only just found its appetite and was far from being sated. M wasn't entirely sure whether it was even the same beast or another of that species, but it operated in a familiar way: it had the same behavior and diet.

Why did M's every thought, every memory, inevitably and rapidly lead her to think about the beast and its workings? When all was said and done it was a discourtesy towards the rest of the world and everything that wasn't the beast, and yet still fully deserved her attention; especially a thing like the circus or the ballet, which was expressly designed to distract the viewer from their own life and not thrust their nose into it, as one might do to a puppy that had left an unwanted puddle. Instead of the old film ending with a celebration of the triumphant collective, M could have been thinking about something different, something more heartening, like the film about the angel who visits a circus and falls in love with the acrobat and who is ready to become an ordinary human creature if it means he can stay with her. But, alas, for all those who came from the place where the novelist had spent most of her life, even the classical ballet—the line of swans in snow-white tutus bending their necks and spreading their winglike arms—was associated above all with shifts in state power, and no one could even remember why.

The grass on the other side of the tarpaulin boundary was lifeless and trampled, worn through in places, the ticket kiosk was empty, even though it was less than an hour until curtain up. A little further away, a group of mechanics in blue boiler suits were busy working on a truck, taking turns to slide under its belly. Outside the tent there was a long makeshift wooden bench, and on it a tin can filled with cigarette butts, and two women of uncertain age who kept bending to brush off their freshly fallen ash. M sat on the other end of the bench, as if to make it clear she was quite alone, lit her own cigarette and watched the lengthening shadows.

She took surreptitious glances at the two women, who were both staring at the ground between their legs as if they'd come to a decision and had no more to say to each other. The woman closest to M was tensed in a physical expression of protest, a weary readiness to resume battle against the state of things. She could have been anything from thirty to forty-five—M had long ago lost the knack of guessing a person's age from their appearance, now everyone always seemed much older or much younger than her, as if she'd reached such a lonely point in her own arc of existence that it was beyond all coincidence with the lives of others. The woman was small, short-haired, with a pointed nose and a cluster of piercings in her pale eyebrows. Her legs in rolled-up shorts attracted M's especial interest: from the skinny ankles upwards, and as far as M could see, climbed a strange tattoo like nothing she had ever encountered. It covered her skin entirely, like a pair of fabulously intricate lace stockings, depicting a pelt of thick curls rising higher and higher towards the groin, as thick and luxuriant as mermaid's scales.

Many years ago, M was shown a medieval sculpture above some German gates. She could no longer remember what it represented, but it could have been a Green Woman, stretched out and so voluptuous it was a delight to behold. Nothing seemed to bother the statue, not the fact that she was naked, nor her legs, which were hirsute and covered in such curls they would have embarrassed any mortal contemporary. Leg hair is an extension of what the Bible calls "uncomely parts" and usually hidden under clothes, as if it were a wild beast, a vixen, desperate to escape and bite everyone. M knew well the ancient story of King Solomon and the Queen of the South who came from far away to study his wisdom. King Solomon of course had other plans for her, the first of which was to tame her, to teach her shame and awe, fear and trembling—in short, to bring her down a peg or two. He had a sort of reservoir constructed in one of the palace rooms, with a layer of thick but quite invisible glass placed over the top and under it goldfish darting about and round-eyed carp swimming through rippling waterweed. When Queen Bilqis was ushered ceremonially into the room by Solomon, she found herself at the edge of this pool and swiftly gathered up her skirts to stop them getting wet, as any of us would have done, and everyone present could see she had hair on her legs. The sight and knowledge of this hair was enough for multitudes of scholars to ascribe to her cloven hooves like a demon's, as well as sexual indiscretion and the desire to follow any young man she was attracted to with the basest of intentions. But, above all, she had given herself away to the King, had placed her animal nature—her beastliness, as it were—on display, and after this she could no more share his throne than she could speak to him as an equal. What a bitter reckoning: all she had wanted was to learn wisdom from a man, about whom she had heard so much; ever since, women have hidden away their shameful body hair, as if it had never existed. The Green Woman, in her shaggy nakedness, was no exception to the rule, in fact rather an emblem of frightful otherness; although in her case this didn't seem to bother her in the least, she was content with the world and her place in it, unlike many of us.

The novelist M was so absorbed by this thought that she didn't immediately notice that a quiet discussion had begun at the other end of the bench, and that she could follow it without straining to understand. The other, younger woman, was talking, and Tattooed Legs listened, swinging her green flip-flops over the baked earth.

"He said we haven't got an act without Lion. It's just a waste of gas," said the younger woman. "I mean, he gets it, and he's sorry and all. Just, he says, he had a contract with Lion, like, he signed Lion, but Lion's dead and buried two weeks already, and there's no one to go out in the ring, so something's got to be done about it."

"Not much can be done about it," Tattooed Legs replied dryly. M wasn't looking at them but she heard the click of a lighter and the long draw of breath.

"He's got someone to replace us, I know it. I mean, like, what's the point of a circus without magic? He'll drop us without a second thought, and we'll be stuck here with all the equipment Lion left behind. What the fuck will I do with that sarcophagus? I haven't even got a place to live. Yeah, right, we'll get our last month's pay but what happens after that? I mean he's hardly going to pay me off for Lion's sake."

"I get it," said the other, and there was silence again. Somewhere beyond the fence an ambulance passed and its piercing siren quickly faded.

"The thing is, the bastard promised me."

"Cohn?"

"Nah. Lion. He promised me he'd make an act just for me. Like, it was three days before he died. Something that wasn't just shaking my ass and waiting to be cut in half. He said he'd teach me a trick, like a memory one, where I get to sit on an antique chair wearing a top hat and tails and guess who's thinking of what card."

They were both silent, all that could be heard was the crunch of gravel under the feet of one of the women who had stood up and was pacing back and forth. She was tall, what might once have been called stately, her eyes prominent in her face, as were her lips. Under her skirt her strong legs were like ancient columns. A thick plait of hair was coiled majestically around the crown of her head. Only her face seemed a little puffy and indistinct, although her large, piercing eyes were outlined dramatically in kohl.

M had been listening to their conversation with great attentiveness—especially as, to her astonishment, it was being conducted in her native language—but it had only just dawned on her that their "Lion" was not the animal from Africa, but a dead human being, "Lion" with a capital L, as it were. She'd missed something crucial at the very outset and now she tried desperately to grasp what they were talking about, as if her own future existence depended on it.

"We'd have got on fine by ourselves, I told you," said Tattooed Legs, as if all three of them knew exactly what she was talking about. "It's not a tricky mechanism, and you must know all Lion's movements by heart after all this time. We just need to find someone to replace you. Come on, stop messing around, let's at least give it a try."

"There isn't anyone," the tall woman replied flatly, as if she'd considered such a step more than once and was convinced it wouldn't work. "No one would do it. And why would they? I mean, you know what Lion was like ..."

"Yeah," said the other after a thoughtful pause. "Lion was a difficult guy to get along with."

12.

M spoke in English to them, as if this was the most natural thing to do in this situation, and in fact it probably was. The problem of language, the "language question," no longer had an acceptable answer and the only way around it was to use English, apparently neutral, mercifully hygienic. Besides, if anyone had issues with English, at least these had nothing to do with the beast that constantly occupied the thoughts of the people from her native country and the countries surrounding it. M couldn't quite work out where the women on the bench came from, but her mouth acted on its own, without her permission, and began shaping and expressing English phrases, and she decided to let it continue for the time being. "Excuse me," said her mouth, "I've just been listening to you and maybe I can help you in some way, or be useful? What needs to be done? What problem do you have?"

The women stared at M, the same astounded expression on both faces, and she shrugged, realizing that her interruption must have seemed at the very least a little odd. "Forgive me," she began again. "I wasn't meaning to listen in to your conversation, I just understood what you were saying. Who are you looking for? An assistant for a magic act?"

The woman with the tattooed legs pushed a half-smoked cigarette into the tin can and turned to face the novelist, studying her with ferocious mistrust. The taller one swung round, shrugged and asked the obvious: "Who are you? What are you doing here?"

"I've come to see the circus," replied M, hurriedly. "I'm here to see the show. But why hasn't it started yet? I've come from G and my connecting train was canceled and they told me there was a circus in town."

The women exchanged glances, they seemed to warm to M—perhaps the absurdity of the situation made them better disposed to her than she really deserved. "There will be a show tonight," Tattooed Legs reassured her. "The box office opens at 8.30. The locals all know the show times, so they won't get here till then. Those posters are all out-of-date."

"Are you performing today?" M asked, hardly knowing why she was persisting with this matter. "Honestly, if you need a volunteer from the audience, I can do it, I don't mind."

The taller woman snorted, looking at her friend as if inviting her to share the joke, but Tattooed Legs did not return her look: she was regarding M appraisingly, calculating her physical capabilities and even her hidden potential. "No, she won't do," said the other in Russian. "She's too tall." "We can always try," Tattooed Legs murmured thoughtfully. "At least we can try," she repeated in English. "Can you get up and walk around a bit? Have you ever done any sports?"

The three of them were sitting together on the bench; a stray yellow dog had even come to join them and was lying on its side, its sleepy paws stretched out. They sat discussing the matter in a language that wasn't their own and wasn't even the language of the country they were in, and their discussion moved slowly towards the as yet unseen sarcophagus and its construction. Soon they came to the point where they needed to take a look at it in order to assess whether it was at all feasible, whether M would be able to carry out this task, so they went around to the back of the tent, pushing their way through the crowds—for now there were people everywhere, swarming around the box office and buying drinks and sugared pretzels at the kiosks. At that moment a trumpet resounded, seeming both remote and very close, calling them to action and readiness.

The sarcophagus was genuinely enormous, disproportionately so, utterly singular and unlike anything else M had ever seen. It was shot through with a seam of dark glass and firmly fixed down on trestles. It appeared to draw the dangerous summer twilight into its body. Round holes had been drilled into the sides, two on the lower part and one on the lid, which could be thrown back with the soft thrum of a spring mechanism, revealing a velvet interior. "Go on, lie down in it," said the younger woman. "On your back, that's right, put your shoulders flat, and now pull your knees up, right up to your chin, just a bit more, a bit more, that's great!" M obediently curled herself up, like an embryo in an old medical illustration, astonished at the way her body responded, as if this position was nothing out of the ordinary and her body was happy to give it a try. "Now turn on your side, but leave your head how it was, can you do that?" Her body, creaking a bit, still managed to draw itself into a tight bundle, but she began to feel cramps in her neck. "Right, we'll shut the box," said Tattooed Legs. The lid fell into place with a soft click. M's head stuck out of the box—there was nothing to hold on to, apart from the pain. The women were checking things, unhurriedly making adjustments, but M couldn't see what they were doing. There was a knock and a click and the lid lifted off. The novelist worked her way back down into the plush lining and twisted her head, trying to make herself comfortable. "Not too bad," said the short-haired woman from somewhere to the side. "I think it could work."

The shadowy room smelled of engine oil and paint thinner. Dresses hung in their covers. From time to time there came the sound of laughter and applause. M lay resting and didn't even turn her head to look. The women were talking together quietly as though they'd forgotten she was even there. "I'll speak to Cohn," promised the tall woman. "Will he refuse?" asked the other. "I'll tell him we've got a replacement. What does he care? He's not going to ask questions. Only we mustn't show her to anyone until we've got the go ahead."

M was in a waking dream in which she was a balloon on a

thread and someone was by turns jerking on that thread and then slowly and agonizingly letting the balloon rise. The ceiling she desired to brush against was unreachably high, but from above, in the dusky light, she could peer down into the open womb of the sarcophagus and see her own body, her knees drawn high and the crooked, almost ratlike line of her mouth. The women were discussing how much they would be paid. Then one of them appeared, almost as if she'd been cut out of the velvet darkness, and told M cheerfully that it was time to get up. M gathered herself and swung her legs down, ready to jump out.

"Not bad," said the short-haired woman. "I think we can work on it. Most important thing to remember is not to twist about, and when you've brought your legs up you need to keep them up, hold them up with all your strength. Do you understand?"

M nodded, blinking sleepily. She felt so at ease, so comfortable that she wasn't yet ready to leave the sarcophagus. Outside the room there was a loud rumbling: not applause, as she'd thought, but actual thunder—a real storm had come over the circus and was shaking the flimsy canvas walls. "You'll come back tomorrow then," the short-haired woman said, "and we'll have another rehearsal, check everything over and then we'll go straight into the performance. It's our last show. We're packing up on Sunday and then we're off, so we only need your help tomorrow. Hey, where are you from then, how come you know Russian?"

The question had once again caught up with her, the second time that day, and would require a proper answer, especially now, with these particular women. But M, who for some reason had no desire to find out where they were from, as if ignorance could protect her from the guilt that stood constantly at her shoulder, said nothing, and simply observed how her body, emboldened and without her conscious involvement, weighed up the possibilities and presented the most carefree, the least truthful, and as it turned out, the most acceptable, answer. "I'm from the South," said her body, giving a nod to indicate the approximate direction and remoteness of this *South*. The answer did not seem to alarm the women or arouse their suspicions. "Who doesn't know Russian," said the woman with the braid, "half of Europe understands it, even if they don't speak it. Are you coming in or are you going to sit out the storm? I thought you wanted to go to the circus? We can get you in, find you a seat. Cohn's program is worth seeing, it's quality stuff. But you will come back tomorrow? You won't let us down?"

13.

In the front row, right next to the ring door curtain, in a delightful new world, and one that was totally indifferent to her, the novelist M fell back into her childhood, or perhaps out of her own self, as a key falls out of a pocket. From outside came the roar of thunder and gusts of wind striking the canvas, but inside there was a great brightness, a glittering, and miracles she could only watch with her mouth agape and her fist pressed against her belly. I don't know what happened in the first half of the show, which she'd spent being measured for her crystal coffin, but in the second half everything was just as when she, as a four-year-old, had been finally allowed into the room to see the festive table, lit with sparklers that reflected off the dark-red glasses of fizzy pop—and the sight made her clap her hands in grateful wonder at the benevolent maternal universe.

A powerful blonde woman in an ornate corset rode into the ring. She performed marvels, vaulting on the back of a white pony; the pony so patiently reliable it might have been a solid little bed on short legs, trotting around in a circle and not in the least hindering its rider from assuming poses or even lying right across its back. Then a helper, a man in black, appeared and began throwing balls to the beautiful blonde rider who caught and juggled them high above her head, while the pony slowed obediently to a walk so the audience could see how cleverly it was all done. Now the lights were dimmed and there was a drumroll and the helper in black ran to the pony, putting blinkers over its eyes, clearly to prevent it from taking fright. Then he began lighting flaming torches, which he tossed to the rider, and she caught them, whirling them through the darkness, juggling one after another until a ring of bright fire had appeared over her head. The people of the town of F applauded all this so loudly as if their delight had reached its peak and nothing more wondrous could be shown to them—and yet there was plenty more to come.

After this, if you can believe it: real lions! M even wondered whether she was still lying in the sarcophagus, dreaming. She was in a civilized country, where the use of animals in circuses was no longer respectable, even in its furthest provinces. But here were genuine, fearsome lions, with huge and powerful paws, and they roared at their trainer as he went from one to the next, commanding them to sit or to lie down or to leap—and then, to the sound of a hushed moan from the audience, he took off his jacket, bent down, and put his head right into the open jaws of the mightiest beast, standing like that for a moment and then withdrawing his head, unharmed. There was ecstatic applause. The lions ran around the ring like clockwork toys and then disappeared, manes and tails and all, vanishing as if it really had been a dream.

This spectacle brought something to mind, vaguely and at the same time quite distinctly, as when you rummage in a bag, knowing both what it contains and what it definitely doesn't (a poisoned snake, say, or the fingers of a pickpocket). M had almost recalled what it was she was groping for in the ragbag of her thoughts when all of a sudden a girl taking tiny steps in tulle-clad legs came rolling out into the ring on top of a huge blue globe. She moved from one corner to another, swaying her body to the music of a fiddle and entirely distracting M from her efforts to remember. Next, some aerial acrobats; M recognized them from the program the tattooed woman had thrust into her hand (together with a phone charger to feed her dormant cell phone back in the hotel). The program had promised many varied delights: acrobats flying high under the dome of the tent; human pyramids; a mind reader. The high point of it all was yet to come, on the following day, when she fully intended to become a vital part of the show herself, embedded at its heart, even if, like the stone at the heart of an apricot, she was ultimately dispensable. But that evening everything the program had promised came true: a strongman in a stripy leotard squatted and then straightened up, bearing on his shoulders the incredible weight of an antique automobile—an impossible feat of strength! An old woman in a shawl called several men and women out of the audience and told them their names and where they came from. Aerial acrobats swam under the dome of the tent like fishes, flying from darkness into light, from trapeze to trapeze; and M herself was transported, filled with a joy, that didn't seem rightfully hers. She couldn't quite dispel the thought that she must be dreaming all these wonders, but when she came out into the night, which bristled and shone like a wet animal, and followed the crowd as it gradually dispersed through the town, her shoes were damp and there was mud stuck to the soles and so she knew it must have been real, that it must have actually happened.

And now she remembered what it was she'd been trying to recall, and even squeaked with joy at the recollection: Imagine a picture that has hung above your bed for many years, a picture of a sleepy wood and a path lit by the sun, and every night as you fall asleep you dream you are suddenly inside this picture and walking down the path, stepping over tree roots, with no idea of where it will lead you. The empty bedroom now lies behind you, and no one back there knows any longer where you are, or even who you are. M had a similar picture in her head—or not really a picture, but a book she'd once read and had forgotten about, in the way that we forget those things we once loved so utterly and gave our hearts to, to love forever. Now the book had once again been opened in her head as if a set of double doors had been thrown back and M stood on the threshold.

It was a children's book, written in verse, one of half a dozen books about a girl who lived in Paris at a boarding school run by nuns, although that didn't stop her from having marvelous adventures, and this was an account of one such adventure. There was a storm in that book, too, a huge and frightening storm, and the little girls from the boarding school were out on a Sunday excursion, on a big Ferris wheel in a fairground, when the downpour began and the wheel stopped. The little girls were put into taxis to be taken home and it was only there they realized that one of them had been left in a tiny yellow cabin at the top of the big wheel, along with her friend, a little local boy. When the nuns returned to the empty fairground the children had, of course, disappeared and no one knew where they had gone.

Everything was in order in the hotel room, the dry shoes by the wall and the useless phone, and the blue bedspread, rucked up like a wave in the center where she had lain a few hours before. No one knew, continued M, as if she were telling a bedtime story, that the little girl and boy in the cabin hanging up in the heavens had been saved by acrobats from a circus; saved and kept warm and given hot drinks and then wrapped in a blanket to sleep for a while. And the next morning the circus set off on its travels and took the children, and they were very happy.

Because circus folk have to earn their keep, the girl and boy were also given a job, and it was one of great honor and importance: the owner of the circus sewed a lion skin for them, it looked just like a real one, and the children put it on before each performance—the little girl at the front and the little boy behind her as the lion's hindquarters (though they must have roared together with one voice). And working as a lion they traveled the world, bathing in fountains instead of baths, fearing nothing and no one, and never ever going to bed before midnight—such lucky children.

M did not care to recall how the book finished—it was a happy ending of sorts, with a homecoming and a cup of warm milk before bedtime. The children didn't seem to mind, the circus folk were grief-stricken but put on a brave face, and if it really was possible to *go home* then M would only have been glad for the young heroes.

But it was "a fact of life" (an expression she'd often heard in her youth) that even if you did go back, it was more than likely you'd find an empty space where your home once stood. Or sometimes it happened that you'd be met with open arms, the milk warming in the pan, and you'd be put to bed, but later that night those who had welcomed you would turn into strange spirits and consume your sleeping figure—so greatly had things changed in your native land while you wandered the world. In short, M had no desire to reflect on homecoming, but the part of the book where the circus appeared and disappeared, crossing borders and traveling the world's highways and byways with the little girl and boy traveling with it, made her feel tender inside. It was just as if she was not the one telling the story, but the one listening to it, holding her breath and clutching onto the hem of her blanket.

And with this, she fell asleep, knowing perfectly well that the charger given to her by the tattooed circus woman was still in her bag on the chair under the window, and that she'd dropped the dead phone into the drawer of the bedside table without plugging it in, thereby doing nothing to reestablish links with yesterday's world.

14.

M slept deeply and dreamlessly—she didn't even have the dream that would have been so appropriate in her situation: the one where she is calmly driving her car along city roads when she suddenly realizes she has no driver license, and that if she were stopped she'd have trouble explaining herself. But on this occasion she lay resting in a velvety black tube somewhat resembling the sarcophagus, and woke alert and ready for adventure. The new day was serene and radiant, as if the tempest of the evening before had washed everything clean. The breakfast room was crowded but she found a table by the window; a handful of hazelnuts from a deep-filled bowl for her oats, some bitter-tasting white yogurt to pour over the top and honey to complete the pleasure. M was hungry yet clearheaded, and the thought of her cell phone, which lay in the drawer next to the Gideons Bible, only made her narrow her gaze like a hawk at the thought of a danger that has been cunningly and calculatingly averted.

It was a kind of childish self-indulgence, this reluctance even to consider glancing at a life she would have to return to sooner or later; just as you might have wallowed in thoughts of suicide or an early tragic death as a teenager, imagining in detail how everyone would mourn and reproach themselves for not having done enough to save you. In a similar vein she liked to imagine that no one, none of the people she knew (and some of these people weren't just acquaintances but were very dear to her), could reach her now, or even imagine what had become of her. This unfamiliar sensation, as if she'd climbed over an invisible wall and had herself become invisible and free, had sharpened the edges of her boundaries and given them a glint of steel another could easily cut their fingers on. She occupied a carefully delineated zone of safety—and even the word "zone" no longer alarmed her. The feeling was akin to stretching out a hand to touch an object, any object, and easily overcoming the distance between it and herself, so that it didn't matter what she did or didn't do: the least action—spreading butter on a roll for example—augured success and anticipated the following step.

A long Saturday awaited her: the best day of all, when the past week was a whole eternity away, and there were hours of freedom ahead—and still another day of liberty to come, unsealed and unwrapped. As M stepped out of the hotel a sea breeze moved the air and caressed her; she had nothing to do until the evening, when the sarcophagus would be waiting for her, the blinding spotlights, even applause. She made her way towards the seashore as she had not yet been there, and she was in F after all, a town particularly known for its coastal location.

But because this new feeling (was it the triumph of self-deception?) was not fully established, but was still young and green in her, M did not walk with the self-possession of a woman who knew everything about herself and where she was going; nor with the gait of a flaneur who doesn't choose the current he floats in; instead she moved in uneven zigzags, stopping to scan every street scene and billboard, searching for clues, for pointers in new directions.

She passed, for example, a series of bus stops, all bearing the same bright ad depicting a man with a dimpled chin, looking out with an expression of reproach—yet as though he hadn't entirely given up hope and still believed things could be mended. The slogan beneath read "Write! Your! Book!" M, who had been full of Saturday spirit and had no desire to write anything, began looking the other way, but the withered-up vestiges of the novelist in her made their presence known through an unpleasant warmth that spread up the nape of her neck.

A sort of dam had formed by an ice cream kiosk: the crowds

moving towards the seafront and the crowds moving away from it slowed and mingled with those lining up for a taste of the cold. A pair of lovers, quite unable to move even a meter or two to the side, kissed pensively, their kisses punctuated by pecks of pink ice cream in narrow waffle cones. M regarded them with indecent interest, slowing down deliberately and noting in herself something like sympathy for the lovebirds. She felt as if these things no longer affected her; the economy of erotic selection and exchange bore no relation to her current existence and this only left her with a sense of relief—as if the obligation to pay off some ancient debt of undisclosed origin had been removed. This didn't stop her from looking at others on the street with (you could say) love in her eyes, following the tilt of a head or the flounce of a skirt. However, this love was fleeting, unfocused, amounting to little more than approval, and was just as likely to be visited on a little stone fountain with a crooked stream as on the movements and forms of her fellow human beings.

Three such fellow beings were standing on the other side of the road, an older woman, a younger woman and a man; the women were wearing patterned frocks, similar in some indefinable way, as if they'd only just bought them in the same shop. The man beside them was young, with a little beard, the sort everyone has now, as if the clocks had gone back to the early twentieth century, before the advent of total catastrophe. As M watched them, he turned to the older woman and quickly and tenderly kissed her hand and then they all crossed the street and disappeared from sight. M decided to turn off the main street, too, and found herself first in one alleyway, then another, until without warning she emerged in front of the inescapable Grand Hotel Petukh with its scarlet windows and white umbrellas. Here, like a windup toy monkey, she did exactly what she had done the day before: she sat at a table, ordered a glass of wine and stretched out her legs to indicate that she was in no rush to go anywhere.

The waitress had a long fringe, gorgeously thick, like a pony's; M could stretch out her legs and even rest them on the edge of another seat and everything felt quite perfect. The sensation of lightness and grace that washed over M had a reassuringly posthumous quality; she felt her body to be made of some glassy transparent material, as if the chairback cover with the emblem of the Petukh could be seen right through her. In any half-respectable novel or film this would have signified that she had already died, en route, perhaps even before she'd reached the town of G, and careful hints to this effect would have been scattered across the body of the text. The novelist M reflected on when, on her journey, her death might have occurred, but she couldn't pick the right moment for it—it could have happened at any time: the toilet of the Turkish café would have provided an amusing backdrop for a heart attack—eventually the café owners would have spotted the blue wheelie bag and wondered who it belonged to—and where the lady traveler had gone. She sipped a little more wine and rearranged her legs, making herself as comfortable as possible.

The man with the ponytail sat down beside her in all his earthly beauty, as if this was exactly where he belonged. He stretched out his limbs and spoke: "I was just walking along thinking I would meet you."

15.

M was not surprised by his appearance nor by his inexplicably warm tone, presumably because she didn't have access to such emotions in her new posthumous existence; there was no time or place for them. She merely moved the glass, the ashtray and her little coffin of cigarettes to one side to show that she had nothing against sitting with him, or possibly even holding a conversation. The waitress with the fringe appeared and took his order, and said it was "a pleasure." For M this foreign language was still a little like someone else's shoes: she put them on, despite knowing full well they were too large for her, the leather stretched by another's foot; but this had its advantages: as a foreigner and an alien she could take everything that was said at face value. She felt a sense of internal excitement at all those automatic expressions like "enjoy!" and "have a nice day!" as if every word of those chance encounters was significant, persuading M both of their sincerity and the truth of these promising forecasts for the future.

They sat at the café table and watched the people passing by—M and the man with the hair clips, who was so unspeakably perfect that under normal circumstances she'd have lost her head and tried too hard to entertain him by chattering aimlessly, or recounting some story, anything to avoid letting the silence fill the space and run over. But she had nothing left, no words and no actions, not even a sense of awkwardness, so she just sat and waited to see what would happen next. Now she could look at him freely, she could see that his hands were unnaturally clean, like the hands of an ophthalmologist or a dentist, and his hair, so neatly confined at his nape, escaped in little strands at his temples. The silence was friendly, even encouraging, it would have been a sin not to spoil it, so when he took his first sip and transferred his gaze to M, she was certain he was about to ask where she came from.

But the man with the hair clips did not ask anything—he was too clever for that. Instead he put his hands behind his head and began speaking clearly and unhurriedly: "I have two tickets for the escape room. Perhaps you'd like to come with me." It wasn't really a question, more a statement of fact and M, in her current composed state, shrugged and answered simply, "Yes."

There was a card in the tarot deck that M had always particularly liked: it was called "Strength," and was usually illustrated with a pair, perhaps a *couple creature*: a woman with a huge lion, both of whom seemed to be o the friendliest of terms. It wasn't clear which party represented "strength," the human female or the wild beast, or the two of them taken together, as it were, but their relationship was manifestly one of real trust. In most cases the maiden holds the lion by the mane or is thrusting apart the lion's jaws, but gently, even lovingly, as if the lion has toothache and needs her help. Sometimes the maiden is perched on its back, and it is wagging its tail like an enormous dog. There is even an ancient Italian deck depicting the woman as preoccupied and unhappy: she stands by a collapsing column, a tragic figure trying with all her might to fix the broken capital back in place as if it could still be made whole. You can see straightaway that it is an impossible task but the lion remains sitting by her feet, a very little lion, not at all frightening, waiting to catch her gaze. And indeed, you might wonder: why bother restoring ancient architecture when you have a real lion?

This last image always reminded M of the illustrations of Saint Jerome, the patron saint of translators, and how we always look for the lion in them and are delighted to find him. Sometimes the lion is tiny, no bigger than a fly, in a far corner of the picture, magnanimously allowing us to forget his presence. Usually the painter gives the animal his due and the clever beast is lying by the saint's feet like a rug, or looking him in the face, seeking his understanding, or trustfully stretching out a paw towards him, with a splinter that needs removing—and of course the saint in his red hat is just about to oblige.

For M, the tarot card "Strength" depicted a similarly comforting symbiosis, only here she could compare herself to the woman and this gave her a sort of satisfaction. If she'd had her own lion she would have treated it with the same care, never messing with its maw unless it was an emergency.

Why on earth was M thinking about all this, while hurrying after the man with the hair clips as he strode towards the mysterious escape rooms they were about to enter? Saint Jerome's monastic quarters were always quite cozy, with the books piled neatly, and a fresh manuscript, which he'd looked up from to exchange a few quiet words with his pet. The novelist M, who was now a person with no known occupation, could only envy the saint, although her own position also had its own unexpected attractiveness. A long, long time ago, in a country that no longer exists apart from on old maps and in history books, the young M sat on a seaside bench early one morning outside a café, which hadn't yet opened, staring avidly at a woman who was crying.

The woman was large, dressed in a strangely glitzy outfit for such an early hour, her hair in disarray. She didn't try to hide the sobs that racked her body in fact, if M remembered correctly, she tapped her sandaled foot in time to their beat. Someone had clearly treated her badly the night before—thrown her aside, or cheated on her, or worse—and her desperation welled up in a rhythmic and powerful pulse, rendering her indifferent to everything happening around her. And M watched her, fascinated, powerless to move or look away; even now she remembered exactly what she had felt back then. It was a mixture of envy and admiration; a sort of stupor in the face of fate; and yet a strange desire to change her destiny and become that very woman. She wanted to howl at dawn while she still had the strength, to feel herself to be in the circus ring as a death-defying feat takes place, all her life focused on that one act.

Back then it seemed to her that this was *it*. That's what I wanted to be, she now thought, meaning: everything all at once, the woman and her uncontainable wailing, the empty café tables—and even now, when she was happiest feeling nothing at all and the last thing she wanted was a pair of invisible hands taking her and wringing her out like wet laundry, she knew which side strength was on and why she, M, had neither lion nor dog.

16.

The concrete building with inexplicably low windows stood behind the Phantorama in a yard. They paid scant attention to the museum itself as they passed it, turning to the left and then the right as if in agreement, although they'd barely exchanged more than a couple of words all this time. M had heard or read a little about escape rooms, already fairly established as popular entertainment, owing perhaps, she thought, to their name, which promised the possibility of a way out at least, if not of flight. When M was a child, her mother told her that a long time ago the signs on the doors of the metro stations in her native city had the terrifying words *There is No Way Out* etched into the glass, as if passengers were being advised to abandon all hope. By the time M had grown up enough to travel on the metro herself, the same prohibition was phrased more usually as *No Exit* or *Closed*, and although it meant much the same, the sense of frightening hopelessness had disappeared—that's how much the choice of words matters.

In escape rooms, however, you had to actively seek a way out, especially given that you'd entered of your own free will and even paid money to do so. M considered this to be not entirely logical, and it felt more than a little risky—reminding her of the famous escape artist who shackled himself in chains, locking the chains with a dozen padlocks before sinking down to the bottom of a water tank. He fully intended to slip off his fetters and swim victoriously to the surface, but something went wrong and he drowned before the eyes of his stunned audience, or at least that's how the legend went, but M couldn't check if she'd remembered it correctly as she didn't have her phone. All these thoughts went through the novelist's head as she stood side-by-side with an unknown man, on the brink of a new adventure, and she would have been happy to share them with him. She can't have had any doubts that he had some sort of plan of action, given that he'd chosen this amusement for them both, and that he'd eventually explain what he wanted from her. Meanwhile their tickets were checked, and they were told that the session lasted sixty minutes, during which time they had to find their way out of the locked room. They were wished good luck and then left to wait their turn in a brightly lit holding area. The man with the hair clips leaned against the wall, half-closing his eyes, and M did not disturb him, although she had plenty to discuss with him.

Still, being left with this pale-eyed man in an enclosed space for a decent length of time was hardly an unpleasant prospect. M looked him up and down brazenly, the way men in the country she came from cast their gaze at passing girls; and he caught this look and grinned, as if he didn't mind being "objectified" in this way. A metal door slid sideways, revealing a bare corridor; once they were inside, it slid shut with a buzzing sound.

"If this was a horror film," said M dispassionately, "I'd turn into a monster at this point and bite your head off."

"If this was a horror film, I'd be the monster—the first victim is always a woman," answered the man with the hair clips.

17.

Every corner of the room was stuffed with hidden clues which needed to be solved one after another, followed like white stones along a forest path that would lead M and her companion to the correct answer and open the door for them. The game's designers had approached their task with enthusiasm and there was no shortage of props, but the actual premise of the puzzle seemed not entirely thought through, and it was hard to work out the general principle, or even what the underlying story might be. But maybe this wasn't necessary to know—it was enough to search for a first clue, leading to another clue and then a third, and so gradually to remove oneself from the stifling clutter of the past, into a world we are used to calling the present.

The interior of the room recalled the hectic energy of a pawnshop's backroom, filled with all sorts of bric-a-brac: an old divan with its sawdust seeping out, a gramophone without a needle, broken televisions, a gynecological chair in the far corner, which made M smile for some unknown reason, some dusty scientific equipment complete with jointed pipes, and, in the middle of all this jumble, a polished wooden desk that the owner of the pawnshop had presumably just abandoned, leaving an open inkwell and a pile of papers. On the top leaf the name of the town of F had been written in large clear letters, together with that day's date. It was clearly a clue, along with the large crystal ball, the type used for seeing into the future, resting on a low table upon a cloth of cherry-red plush. The glass appeared clouded, but the ball was not covered by a layer of dust, unlike most of the surrounding objects.

Her pale-eyed companion approached the task methodically,

energetically opening all the drawers and checking under the seats of chairs. A cabinet revealed a plastic classroom skeleton wrapped in a bicycle chain, and a few jars of preserved eels.

M, too, picked up and examined a beer tankard with an emblem on it she didn't recognize, leafed through an ancient album of stickers lying out in pride of place (Marlene Dietrich in scarlet, stuck next to Leni Riefenstahl in blue) and got quickly bored. She sat down on the old divan, avoiding the rusty spring that poked through the fabric. Her companion clearly didn't need her help, but perhaps by talking to him she could keep him alert, like a driver in danger of falling asleep at the wheel. He was digging through piles of books, opening each one and carefully shaking it out. Sometimes all she could see was his back and his by now familiar shoulder blades—only here she could stare at them openly. All of a sudden he said something, but she missed it and asked him to say it again. "No," he said, "grandmother would not have liked it here. Or maybe she would. Difficult to say."

To begin with, M wondered if this was a figure of speech: maybe in this part of the world a reference to "grandmother" was a kind of ice breaker? But no, this grandmother seemed to be real enough, a genuine grandmother, and still living. "I wanted to bring her here," said the pale-eyed man. "I thought she'd be entertained by it. She likes games and solving things. I often buy her puzzle books. And she'd have found digging around in all this old stuff interesting, I guess. It might have brought back memories. She doesn't go out anymore, hasn't for the last six months, but before that we used to do a lot together. I used to take her to cafés—there's a nice one up on the hill. I thought she'd like this as well."

M asked the grandmother's age, as was expected of her, and the man with the hair clips answered readily enough that she had just had her 102nd birthday. She was in an old people's home and he often came to F to visit her, so that's what he was doing there.

"She's had a hard life," he added, and looked at the novelist as if in reproach, or perhaps it just seemed that way to her.

"I can imagine," said M, "with a date of birth like that. Quite the century she's had."

"She doesn't want to live anymore," said the pale-eyed man, "she wakes up every morning and says: *Not dead again, still fucking here.*"

"They usually want to go home," said M, who had some experience in this matter.

But the pale-eyed man's grandmother didn't want to go *home*, and this set her apart from the other old people. She wanted to die as quickly as possible, but she couldn't make it happen. Before she'd been put into the very good care home she had twice tried to take her own life but it hadn't worked.

"One time," said the man with the hair clips—he'd stopped shaking out books and was squatting in the midst of all the bric-a-brac, in front of the disintegrating divan and looking directly at M—"she took pills, a whole lot of them, eighty in all, and they found her completely by accident. There was a leak in the apartment below and they knocked on her door, and she was just lying there. So she was taken to hospital and resuscitated. She tried again six months later, but failed on that occasion, too: someone in the family called her and she didn't pick up. They called the police and the police broke her door down, took her to hospital, and resuscitated her. Now I'm the only one in the family she talks to. She can't forgive us for saving her."

"She didn't do it right," M blurted out. "At home anyone can ring you or just arrive at your door. You need to go to a hotel, a Holiday Inn or something, where they have hundreds of people staying and no one could care less about you. Check in, go up to your room, and hang a sign on the door: do not disturb. That would be a much, much better way."

She stopped, realizing what she'd said, and fell silent.

The fact that they had been speaking in English all this time, a language that belonged to neither of them, gave the proceedings a faintly oneiric quality altogether fitting for a room without windows, piled high with homeless objects, including the still inscrutable crystal ball. On the other hand many people now expressed themselves in a foreign language every day, inhabiting it, adapting it to their needs and finding refuge not in the words themselves but somewhere in between them, so that reality itself seemed like a dream in which you are traveling endlessly on a train or a plane or a bus, standing in passport lines or looking over heads in a waiting room while your flight is repeatedly delayed and you are never able to reach your destination. And that is for the best, because you can no longer remember where you are going, nor what you left behind.

"I wonder," said M, to change the subject, slightly unsure what would be an appropriate topic of conversation, "if it's not all a bit simpler than it looks. It wouldn't surprise me if you just had to take that bit of paper with the writing on, heat it over the candle and a secret text will appear. We used to do that when I was a child, we'd write messages in milk on paper."

The man with the hair clips shrugged, but did nothing. He stayed sitting by M's feet, watching her as if she herself were the clue. Something had changed in the air between them, and now it was M who stood and began busying herself, rummaging frantically through the pieces of a construction kit in a cardboard box—enough to make a little house, or a whole railway station. The being that had watched her from the beginning of the journey, at times from within, at times from without, was now somewhere up on the ceiling, looking down at her with pitying condescension; she was regressing, turning into her usual self, herself from before yesterday; her only course of action: to take a tumble down the stairs, or to drop some heavy item with a clatter, so as to cover over one embarrassment with another. Sensing this, the novelist came to a halt.

"You know what," she said, after a moment. "If I light a cigarette the fire alarm will go off and they'll open the doors and let us out."

"That will cost us more than the tickets themselves," the pale-eyed man observed reasonably.

At that very moment the lightbulb blinked, signaling the end of their session. The door buzzed and a woman appeared and offered them an extra fifteen minutes, but they refused this, even though it was not very sporting of them.

18.

They sat under a canvas awning, dipping spoons in bowls of cucumber soup, with the carefree demeanor of people who have finished their work and can now give themselves up to the pleasures of the day. After all, they'd found a novel way out of a hopeless situation, without needing to dig through books or drawers or answer riddles. It had been enough to do nothing, simply to wait for the situation to resolve itself. It was, according to the man with the hair clips, the most economical approach and therefore the optimal one.

But M had her doubts. She'd lived her whole life like this, doing nothing, or doing only what came naturally to her, and wanting to believe she had got away with it. This approach, to judge by her current position, clearly did not suit all circumstances.

Nevertheless, she was enjoying eating lunch with him in the sea breeze, without having even asked his name or where he'd come from. That, at least, she didn't need to ask: the answer was clear, the pale-eyed man was about the most local person she could have come across, he was from this very town; his grandmother's presence here only confirmed this. M didn't fully understand what he was up to—the purpose for his visit to the town of F might be clear, but what was he doing here with her: a vague, indeterminate creature, stained with disgrace? The infection was perhaps not outwardly visible, but her companion was attentive and must have felt intuitively that something was not right with her. However, he showed no sign of this and acted as if nothing at all was the matter; he was calm, careful, and he, too, asked no questions.

Between the soup and the main course of stuffed mushrooms,

M had a brief but clear vision of being alone with the man in a closed and hidden room, a little more comfortable than the escape room with its dusty exhibits, much like her own hotel room in fact, with a bed cover in the same blue. M shook her head to dissipate this insistent image and began talking about Peter Cohn's circus. Her companion had never been, and appeared to disapprove of circuses in general, their unsophisticated style of entertainment. But he listened tolerantly enough to M's enthusiastic descriptions without objecting or making ironic remarks, and she in turn did not speak of the narrow bed inside the sarcophagus that awaited her—partly in gratitude, partly in self-interest, not wishing to scare him off before it became inevitable.

M had democratic tastes, even if she didn't always have time to indulge them. She liked Christmas fairs, with tourists trampling the snow around kiosks, and glühwein, and nuts coated in cinnamon and sugar, and funfairs at night with colored lights, and roller-coaster cars squealing into the abyss, and twirling swans as big as the ones on the lake where she lived. She was fond of ice cream and boating on lakes and little river ferries slipping under low bridges, with someone always waving to them from the parapet above, like God, who has noticed, and blesses you from on high. It wasn't that she endlessly partook of all these activities, it was simply enough that they existed, and at such proximity she could reach out and touch them.

Over the last year M had begun to have doubts about these pleasures, all so various and yet so similar in every country she traveled to. If in the past she'd enjoyed their openness and indiscriminate appeal—for anyone to enjoy, and needing no special preparation to participate—now she remembered the winter ice rink in the city where she no longer lived, the lights of its coffee shops at night, and with a shudder she wondered whether those she'd shared the frosty air with were now killing others in a foreign land, where the coffee shops stayed open as the air raid sirens sounded, and every family kept a record of their fallen. It felt as if joy itself was now prohibited, its pure essence muddied with traces of blood. Even though M often reminded herself that joy was the very thing the beast was bent on annihilating, in her own and other neighboring countries, and that it was important to keep it alive to spite the beast, she hadn't until then succeeded in following her own advice. On the previous evening, however, something had changed in her or around her—though she had hardly got used to this new quality in her life and wasn't even sure it would last. This is why she looked so expectantly at her new companion, as if at a gift still in its box. He looked over at her palm, lying flat on the table like an abandoned reticule, and stretched out his own large hand, but didn't touch hers, simply held it half a centimeter above hers, so she could feel its warmth. He stayed like that until she lifted her eyes to look at him, and she didn't lower them again.

"I'm leaving tomorrow evening," said the man with the hair clips. "My train is at five. I'll be in B by eleven. Shall we travel together? What do you think?"

They had a common future, or so it seemed, one she could inhabit for a short time. If this was a book—her book—the novelist M would've done everything in her power to slow things down, because everything was going far too well; it was all too neat, and the unnatural ease of events made the heroine feel certain there was trouble ahead. But this was actual real life, and so M exhaled cigarette smoke and said cheerfully that she would be glad to.

Something had begun to worry her though, something was not quite right, obliging her to *ask a question*, and she was not ready to do so. The medieval novel that she had been brought up on, so to speak, taught the reader that questions should be asked instantly, without delay, as soon as they began to take shape. The courteous young hero of the book, who considered it honorable never to express surprise or ask any questions, found himself in strange circumstances that should have led him to ask his hosts if they were in trouble and needed his help, but, for the sake of good manners, he held his tongue. The result of this was that the castle where he had spent the night was swallowed up by the earth, together with its inhabitants, and it was all the fault of the young knight. If he'd asked only one question they would have been saved, and not just his hosts, but all of humanity; instead, centuries of torment awaited them, continuing to this day. M imbibed the uncomplicated ethical message of this text as a teenager, but now it seemed that she had got it all wrong; she was swelling like a balloon, holding in big painful gulps of fevered breath—anything was preferable to asking the simple question: how did he know she lived in B and would be going back there?

She must have given herself away with a sudden movement, or involuntary sound, and the man with the hair clips and the pale eyes said very simply, as if it hardly mattered, "Well, I do know who you are, I recognized you on the train, although I didn't immediately realize it was you." The word "you" began to occur in his speech with threatening frequency, and M shivered as if she felt a sudden chill. He explained that he'd been at a literary festival not long ago where she'd appeared, and M briefly wondered if that was worse than him reading one of her books. But no, there was not much difference, both scenarios seemed as bad as each other. Those curtained-off images that had inhabited her head over the last hour or so were incompatible with a reader, they became entirely inappropriate. So it was not about her at all, not about M, but a traveling novelist from a far-off country who had kindled in him a respectful interest, and this had been enough to leap over everything that divided them and bring them to this shared table, the closed room, and God knows what else. The blue bed cover momentarily billowed like a sail on a boat, then faded to nothing. He mentioned her recent book by name—so he was her reader!—and M steeled herself for cultural dialogue.

In the house by the lake, where she'd been living these past months, there was a community of people, artists and intellectuals, gathered from all around the world to work on their projects and in their free moments to sit and exchange opinions. To this end there was water and swans and daily lunches, where everyone met to eat and chat. The novelist M had made a few friends and while they were talking about opera or the local food everything was fine. But sometimes the conversation turned to current events, and M still remembered how someone there had begun explaining to her that she was too critical of her own great country, being herself unambiguous proof of its achievements. "The contemporary world levels everything," her interlocutor declared. "Only in authentically conservative societies do you find a place for genuine otherness, which distinguishes one culture from another. Yes, culture is a bloody business," he added, not without pleasure. "Take Iran for example—we all adore Iranian film directors, but where would they be if the religious state didn't stand in the way of globalism? Of course there are sacrifices, but what if great art can only happen against a backdrop of great violence? It's time we accept that it's a prerequisite—and in that sense you've forged ahead of us over the last few years."

That day M sat for a long time on a bench near the lake, so concealed by bushes that from a distance she was invisible. She ran through all the possible rejoinders in her head, finding no single unsurmountable objection to the statement. The simple "you shall not murder," to which all her thoughts returned, was, in this case, of little use. Her opponents' thinking was of a more Olympian order, and the distance that separated them from the places where war was being waged meant they could treat M and those like her as objects in a vacuum, entities in an ongoing experiment they observed from a detached position. However the experiment turned out, the results would be of some scientific interest. They could busy themselves thinking about cultural variety in the world, "troubled societies," like the one the novelist M came from, making any number of curious observations about human nature and what it might be capable of when subjected to extraordinary conditions. Much was expected of M in this regard: she might offer insights, illuminating the wider history of the issue without neglecting the local detail, which few outsiders knew much about. The women's situation was of special interest of course, and she, as a woman and a witness, was expected to write about this.

Fortunately M was no longer a novelist, even if she tended to keep quiet about this in polite society—because if she wasn't a novelist, then what was she? During the brief time she'd spent in F she had begun to test, like dipping a toe in the ocean, her ability to be no one, but she hadn't reached the point where she felt at home in this water—and then reality had suddenly yanked her by the collar and commanded her to sit and talk, and M obeyed—what else could she do now she'd been exposed?

The reader was tactful and prepared. M still didn't know his name and he knew a great deal if not everything about her, and the asymmetry troubled her, although as before she didn't want to ask him any questions. He began by saying that he understood how difficult it must be for her, and he asked a perceptive question about the situation in the country she had once lived in. Such interest should have pleased her, but she was mourning the past few hours when they had both been people without provenance, without a long train of circumstances that needed to be taken into account. She answered his questions languidly and reluctantly. He now knew everything about her and she knew nothing about him; the fact he had a fierce grandmother with a difficult life did little to help. You see, M had thought for some reason that he'd liked her as she was, for herself, an unknown woman at a café table, and it was as if this new turn of events had put out a light inside her. They finished their coffee, said goodbye almost without awkwardness, and agreed to meet the following day by the station taxi rank. Then the man with the hair clips disappeared around a corner as if he had never existed.

19.

M returned to the hotel and, like that man on his business trip, lay down immediately on the blue bedspread without undressing or looking in the mirror. In any half-respectable book about a female novelist running away from her responsibilities without telling anyone where she's gone, retribution would be sure to catch up with the heroine, and now it was clear precisely what form that would take: the tall blond-haired man with the overly neat ponytail should have strangled her in the escape room, on the divan with the spring sticking through, and then in mysterious fashion escaped from the locked room—that would make an excellent opening scene for a detective novel. M's story would be short but edifying. In such a plot she wouldn't even be the heroine, merely the first victim, but surely that was no more than she deserved?

The day shone bright, and then slowly tipped towards its end as M lay on the bed.

If she'd had a lion's pelt on her back and only the vast miles of scrubland around her then she could have bitten off the beautiful head of the pale-eyed man, who really didn't know who he was dealing with: not, in any case, with "the novelist M," but with a new being, just M, or maybe A, still fresh and instinctive, and ready for adventure. He'd mistaken her for another, and wasn't even capable of hiding this, and now she felt rage inside—but who was this rage directed at? And which of her personas had it came from?

The mistake was an innocent one, but there was so much guilt around M, and in her, that it was hard to breathe; you could suffocate in all that guilt, and perhaps that had already happened and the hotel room with its expanse of windows was in fact a preserving jar, with M inside, pickled in her own guilt, and others' guilt, covered in thick rat fur, holding one paw to the sky. In any case she still had some unfulfilled promises hanging over her head, made rather rashly in a moment of sudden freedom, and it was time to honor these. She began to stir, reluctantly, creaking and groaning on the bedcover. The New Being was apparently unwilling to show itself; it had been displaced by misery in her no-longer-young body, which lay idle and protesting, resisting every command to get up and keep going.

Peter Cohn's circus trembled slightly under the heat of the sun like a mirage. The women, almost indistinguishable from each other to begin with, waved to her from the bench, slowly becoming more distinct as she approached.

"We thought you weren't coming," said the one with the braid.

20.

She entered the shadowy room where the sarcophagus lay as if she were coming home; home as in back to the hotel room, that is, a place where all the elements were familiar to her and gave her a pleasant sensation of order. Although there was nothing of order in M's surroundings now, and definitely not in her head, where a single phrase repeated itself as if on a loop—she wanted to say it out loud, joyfully and triumphantly like a ringmaster announcing the next act, and she thought how very funny it would sound: *not dead, yet, I'm still fucking here*. And she'd open her arms wide, *ta-da!* But both the women, the short-haired one and the one with the braid, looked serious today, almost severe, as if they wanted to fill M with a personal sense of mission, or else the appropriate level of fear, before the trial that awaited her. She had to make an effort to hide the weightlessness of her existence from them: it was as if she'd come unattached from the earth over the last few hours and could even slip through walls or drift up under the dome of the tent—or perhaps she just needed to eat and her hunger had rendered her transparent and heedless. Two pairs of identical fiery red goatskin boots stood by the wall. They hadn't been there the day before, but otherwise everything was as she'd remembered it, and the sarcophagus lay open and inviting.

M took her place in the velvet womb and readily brought her knees up to her chin. It wasn't hard, only boring and painful, to lie with a twisted neck while the woman with a braid counted time. It lasted longer than the day before; they went through it twice, then once more, and then again. M had to climb out of the sarcophagus and stand a little way from it afterwards, as the short-haired woman was also part of the act and had to lie curled up at M's feet and do some extra tricks they hadn't mentioned to M. They practiced the same thing again, but this time with both of them, and then once again from beginning to end. All the events of the last few days had begun to double and triple, lying in untidy layers one on top of another so that what was happening now seemed quite natural, especially as she was thinking of something quite different: she now wanted to know how the escape room worked, what puzzles they would have needed to solve to get out if she and the pale-eyed man hadn't just been killing time in there and had done everything properly.

"So have you got it all then? We don't need to run through the whole thing again?" The woman with the braid, leaning over the side of the sarcophagus, spoke in a chant: "Come out—stop—bow to the left—bow to the right—stop—now come over *and* legs up straightaway—lie down—smile. I'll shut it up—drumroll—you get ready—hold your legs—keep your head straight—we'll do the trick and you lie there—smile—keep your neck straight—sarcophagus goes on its end—you immediately put your legs down and straighten up—lid goes back—smile and wave—and that's it, you're pushed offstage."

"You need to get changed," said the shorter woman flatly. She'd already climbed out of the box and stood there in a T-shirt and shorts; she didn't appear to need any extra props.

M suddenly felt very aware of her jacket and trousers, fine for a train journey or the Phantomoteke but quite out-of-place in the blazing light of Peter Cohn's world, and she was even more ashamed when she thought of her body, still working, still obeying her, but hardly the physique of a circus performer. She remembered the horseback rider in her gorgeous corset and the blue tulle-clad girl on the ball, taunting in her slimness. M moaned softly in shame.

"The dresses are over there," the taller woman nodded in the direction of the clothes, their fabulous forms faintly visible under the opaque hanging covers.

M went over to the clothes and tugged on the first one's zipper; the opening revealed a tiny swan costume, innocent white gauze with a feathery fringe. "You really think that would suit me?"

The short-haired woman was rifling through the dresses, looking for the one she had in mind. It seemed there was no choice after all; M would take whatever she was given. She was presented with a long red dress that reached down to the floor, like something an opera diva might wear, and exactly the same fiery color as the boots in the corner—they were clearly meant for each other. Like at a doctor's appointment when you shed your clothes, leaving them on a stool behind the curtain, to emerge as if made new, M stripped and dived headfirst into the crimson silk. It rustled up to meet her, chilly to the touch. The absurd-looking boots were a size too large, and M, unaccustomed to such high heels, staggered as she stepped forward towards a mirror under a dim lightbulb.

The tall woman appeared at her side and put an object into her hand, something so wildly beyond her imagination that at first M didn't know what to do with it. It was a headdress, covered in metallic scales, with feathers sewn onto a fabric cap, which fitted tightly around the skull like a stocking. It took the two of them to get it on her, but when M at last looked into the mirror she saw with a shiver that her wish had come true. The being that stood in front of her had nothing in common with the former M, nor with any of the Ms she could have imagined. Of course, she often wanted to hang her old obsolete self on a hook and spring into the world as a different person, like a cuckoo from a clock—but the imagined new version looked much the same as the novelist M on closer inspection, just a sleeker, smarter, unnaturally energetic upgrade with a ready wit; refreshed by long anesthetizing sleep and having shed all its old phantom pains like a lizard's tail. The long figure in red reflected in the mirror did not look like her, indeed it hardly looked like a human at all. The feathers stuck out and swayed, the sequins flashed, and you could hardly make out the human face beneath, all its features were lost. A tube of crimson silk descended to where two red hooves protruded. Only the arms were hers, hanging at her side as if they'd been stitched on, and M hesitated, unsure what to do with them.

Then they all went out into the dark air of the yard behind the tent, M taking tiny steps, the women flanking her watchfully and they lit up cigarettes while they still had the time and space to smoke.

Once, on a summer's evening in a beautiful foreign city, M had wandered to the foot of the tower for which the city was famed. The tower was illuminated, and people sat on the grass around it as though they were watching it from in the stalls of a theatre. Some had brought picnics and cool drinks, staring at the tower for all the world as if it was a ballet performance. Others were even making videos of it simply standing there in its bright splendor. A little further away from the tower, and enfolding it, was the soft dark interior of a park, with alleys and benches, pruned hedges, and the crunch of gravel underfoot—but the gathering visitors hadn't come here to dive into the welcoming green twilight. The tower strove towards the heavens like a huge brooch: a monstrous and disproportionate many-faceted twinkling thing. Around it light sparked, smoldered, and flowed, and there was nowhere to hide from its white-hot intensity. Even in the darkness of the park, tiny pinpricks of light seemed to tick and glow. African street traders squatted on the ground with their wares laid out on cloths before them, but these, too, were copies of the same tower—some bigger, some smaller—all blinking and flashing like a jar of fireflies or a Christmas tree, or Europe at night under the belly of a plane, and it made M's head spin. Others went from tree to tree offering souvenirs to bystanders, and from their belts hung towers, endless towers, dozens of them, glowing with phosphorescent light. Everything around was light-bearing, even the straps on the sandals of the girls standing at the corner gleamed with a scattering of diamonds. M shut her eyes as if she was being scalded.

But really, what can be expected of someone, M thought in the last moments before she went on stage (she could see how the tall girl with the braid was nervous, dressed in a black frock coat, which was large, even on her), what can honestly be expected of a person who seems to think that all it takes is to reappear in the world, to walk among people, thinking that will solve things. You'd only have to open your eyes to see what a mistake that was. The one thing that can bring relief is complete and lasting darkness, soothing and unchanging darkness, without dreams or hope or any other distraction. But at that moment applause resounded, the curtain lifted—and there was light.

The light was overwhelming, as it had been at the illuminated tower. She walked, swaying on her heels, as if inside a chandelier of preposterous dimensions, with hundreds of candles and thousands of eyes, and everyone wriggling with excitement and applauding wildly. To her left was the matte blue-black sheen of the sarcophagus. The tall woman cried out in a ringing voice, addressing the audience with a few distinct phrases, and the audience was spellbound: *Death-defying!* (this was repeated a few times) and *Right now!*

M bowed to the left and the right as she'd been instructed ("like a highwayman on the scaffold," said a voice in her head) and watched the lid of the sarcophagus slide off, revealing her velvet roost. Two assistants ran in towards the tall illusionist, one bringing a pair of white executioner's gloves with a wide cuff, and she began pulling them on, glancing anxiously at M, who was taking her time for some reason. The other assistant carried a case, rather like a cello case, and began unfastening the straps. When he finally opened it, it turned out to be holding a hefty chainsaw with ferocious teeth.

M sighed and climbed into the sarcophagus.

It's not that she hadn't guessed that the act she'd been brought in to help with involved being sawed in half. Just that the details of the procedure hadn't been discussed with her, and the picture she'd had in her head was somehow vague, and based on a distant memory of meniscus surgery when she'd had only a local anesthetic and, but for a little curtain, could have watched the surgeon working his magic on her injured knee.

She lay her neck in the cutout hole and waved her feathers in fond farewell. The sarcophagus was reminiscent of Snow White's crystal coffin in a picture book, just before the prince came to wake her with a kiss. Nothing seemed more ridiculous to M at this moment than a kiss, and she felt slight bewilderment when she remembered her conversations with the pale-eyed man and the candle flicker in her stomach at his presence. How quickly it had all faded. Deep in the sarcophagus below her feet, she could feel something going on, the short-haired woman was waiting there. The boot on M's foot slipped, and M twisted her toes up to keep it in place, but to no avail.

The lid slid smoothly forward and closed with a sucking sound and at the same moment the chainsaw began its shriek: the snub-nosed illusionist was walking around the edge of the ring, demonstrating her terrifying instrument to the audience and distracting them, so M could do her work. The woman then returned to the sarcophagus and inserted a thin panel, and then a second panel, into deep slits in the sarcophagus, marking the place where the saw would pass through.

M lay twisted up under the lid, sweating, wearing only one boot and smiling heroically as she had been instructed. There was a muttering of drums. It was a proper high-quality circus, as she already knew, with all manner of special effects, and the ring was now in complete darkness—only the sarcophagus was lit up, like a blue torch.

There were people standing close by; she could hear them

breathing, but couldn't see them clearly. The woman with the braid was also out of sight, moving somewhere beyond the glassy body of the sarcophagus. The chainsaw coughed, squealed, made its grating, rattling noise, and the sarcophagus shook violently. And then it was all over, the ground was moving under her, and M could see one of the assistants, who seemed to be very far away, wheeling the other half of the sarcophagus around—with two red boots hanging out from its end.

21.

The audience clapped and clapped as if the terrible death-by-chainsaw and the miraculous reunion of the two halves of human flesh were the highpoint of the whole evening: the long awaited good news of the resurrection. If the novelist M had still been with us she would have recalled yet another story, one in which they brought the hero back to life after his body was chopped into pieces by villains. A common enough motif, she might have added, but this particular version was curious in its approach. All the pieces of the unfortunate body had to be gathered first—all the dismembered parts that had been scattered wide over the steppe—brought to one place and impelled to become one flesh again. Two vials of water were then brought to the corpse; in one the water of life and in the other the water of death. The dead man's body was sprinkled with the water of death and every part then returned to its rightful place, the body repaired its wounds, its lost integrity was restored. The water of life could now take effect—and, look!—the eyes opened and could see, and the limbs that had been cut apart were filled once again with living warmth, the hero stood on his feet and was *like new*, quick with life, and there the story ended. But M was no longer with us to explain how it had all worked, only the noise of the applause that seemed never-ending; and someone's child in the front row screaming, "Again! Do it again, please!"

M was just at this moment stretching out her numb body parts and the littler woman was doing the same, climbing at last out of the sarcophagus and stamping her tattooed legs in their red boots assiduously. "We did OK," she said encouragingly to M. "No worse than when Lion was doing it."

They sat on the bench in the now silent wasteland, drinking the short-haired woman's schnapps from a flask. M was barefoot, still wearing the long dress, and her partner still wore the red boots and shorts. The tent gave off warmth and the pleasant scent of animals, but the ground beneath the soles of her feet was already cooling, readying itself for the night. In the distance, and hardly visible, lights twinkled in the windows of houses on the hill and the rear lights of cars blinked past on the road that led out to the autobahn. M could easily have fallen asleep leaning against the warm shoulder of her companion; she was faintly surprised that it was still Saturday, the day had truly lasted an eternity, but just then the beautiful woman with the braid appeared and said that Peter Cohn wanted to speak with her.

Peter Cohn, the owner of the Peter Cohn circus, was not at his own show that night. He was sitting under a bright lamp in dark glasses. M greeted him and sat down without being asked, as her legs no longer seemed to want to hold her up.

He was a small man, reminding her of the incense-burning figurine from her childhood: dark green, the size of her little finger with a tiny straw wedged into its mouth that, set alight, would make it puff out scented smoke. Cohn sat in a canvas armchair and a sturdy walking stick with a carved tiger's head handle was leaned against it. He either couldn't or didn't want to speak English, and so M spoke to him in the local language that she knew only approximately and was ashamed of her stilted speech. But he didn't seem to care about her mistakes or her embarrassment, possibly because people who allow themselves to be cut in half by chainsaws or who are ready to walk along high wires hanging right up in the heavens, were often foreign and communicated as well as they could without worrying too much about cases and declensions.

"I heard you didn't do too badly," said Cohn and frowned. "Have you done this before?" M answered that she hadn't. A little way off one of the lions roared, and after a moment there was applause.

"What is your name, my dear?"

He was the first person on her journey who had asked not where she came from but what she was called, as if this was important and M lifted her face to him from the low chair where she sat and answered honestly and without giving it any thought, that her name was A.

"Here's the thing," said Cohn. "Tonight was our last show. Tomorrow we travel on. Your friends need an assistant and they're unlikely to find one. If they don't, we shall have to part ways. I can't keep people on if they are of no use to me. But I think that a few months' work might be of interest to *you*, am I correct?"

M hadn't expected this turn of events. She sat and listened without speaking.

"I have no idea what has happened in your life and I won't ask. It's none of my business. I don't pay much, you aren't worth it yet, but you would have a roof over your head," he pointed at the canvas ceiling, "and food. I'll pay for all that. We travel around Europe, so you won't have to get out your passport, don't worry. We'll have a week or two in N, then we'll be off again, on to somewhere else. The work isn't difficult. Would you like to come with us, my dear?"

"This is quite unexpected," replied M in the unfamiliar tongue. "I need to think."

"You can have until tomorrow," said Peter Cohn. "We're leaving at eight. Be here by seven in the morning, and we'll find you a place in one of the trailers." And then added, without turning his head towards her, and with slight emphasis, as if reading her palm, "No, you aren't Romanian."

M, who had never once in her life pretended to be Romanian, stared at him and opened her mouth, and suddenly knew, clearly and absolutely, that the question of who she was and where she was from had at last been put to her—although not in the form she disliked most—and that she now had to give an answer, to say where she was born and how she'd reached these parts, and what she thought about this, even if no one had asked her yet. She had an answer, she stirred in her chair and prepared to speak—but Cohn was not listening. Sitting about two meters away from her, he began sniffing the air between them, even tilting his head slightly, like a dog trying to understand. She saw her shadow on the wall and realized she was still wearing the headdress, that scaly stocking with the stupid feathers stuck in it, and she pulled it off quickly, hardly daring to wonder how she must have looked all this time, and what Cohn must have made of her.

"No, you're not Romanian," he repeated, and the big lamp was reflected in both lenses of his dark glasses. "My dear. you're *ex nostris*. You're a Jew, aren't you?" And M, who for the last months had only ever referred to herself as a Russian, a Russian novelist, a speaker of Russian, replied almost with astonishment, that yes, she was—yes.

When she got up to go, Peter Cohn did not get out of his chair, that was not his way. Instead he pointed with his carved stick at the door, but not at the door itself, somewhere just to the side of it, and it was only then that M realized her new employer was blind.

22.

Those who have not acquired the habit of rising early, or who have never needed to do so for work or any other reason, rarely see the light of dawn, and every time they do, it feels like an undeserved gift, or a reward for an inadvertent achievement: the empty streets, the crimson and still sleepy sun caught in the trees suddenly becoming an extraordinary spectacle—and the lucky novice there to peep at it all.

In the house on the lake, M often saw the dawn from the other side when the night softened, the water beginning to glint, and the first empty bus rumbling past her balcony towards the city. This was the same sense of peeping, but of a different, guiltier order, like dallying in a place where you shouldn't have been and seeing what you shouldn't have seen. And it was true she whiled away the nights fecklessly, doing nothing of importance. If she'd felt even a small sense of being needed, or useful, as when she was still a novelist, then everything would have been different, she thought, but now sleeping and not sleeping resembled each other: both left the vexing taste of time passed that wouldn't come again.

Long before, in a different place and time, she had loved getting up early to go to the airport or the railway station, feeling both a tautness and a sense of purpose in her gut and in her gaze—as when you have set yourself a goal knowing you have the means to achieve it. In the winters back then the snow lay on the boulevards and pink light shone from the windows of the few cafés that were still open. In the spring everything looked as if it had been scrubbed clean and smartened up—even the absence of people on the streets seemed to promise an event of some sort, like the twice-yearly festive marches that took place when she was a child to celebrate the workers. Enterprising traders sold rare treats on those marching days: cockerel-shaped lollipops, special double balloons—one balloon ingeniously housed within the other and both filled with helium—or little flags with the slogan: *Peace! Labor! May!* The marchers proceeded down the empty Peace Prospect to rousing music that made one's chest swell like the singing of choirs. They held armfuls of plastic flowers, huge red poppies and bare branches with buds glued to them, cut from tissue paper in the colors of early spring.

Children were allowed, and even encouraged, to pester the marchers with calls—"Hey, give us a flower!"—and the little M frequently came home with a whole skirtful of incorruptibly fake flora. She loved it all so much she couldn't sleep the night before and would get up before dawn and run out onto the street, where still nothing had happened, no traders or music or grand processions, only the first ice cream vendors, setting up their stalls on the street corner. One thing M couldn't understand was the indifference, even slight hostility, her parents showed to these spring and autumn days marching under a banner. They didn't appear to want to accompany their daughter outside, or to buy her everything her heart desired—and if they did go out, they did it with such reluctance that even as a child she could sense it.

There was a time when she felt a sort of pride in getting up as early as possible and leaving the house long before she needed to; trudging to school in the blue winter dawn, scuffing up the snow with her warm boots and watching it spark in the beams of the infrequent streetlamps. The morning's broadsheets had already been pasted on the boards, but you could barely see through the lit windows, as they were covered in complex patterns of ice, as dense and impenetrable as tropical forests. The anxiety that gripped her that year had no focus or cause; day after day she would arrive at the deserted school an hour or more before she needed to be there.

She liked the empty corridors, with the portraits and timetables on the walls, the cloakroom with its bristle of coat hooks, and the only coat in there: hers, for the time being. The building was a hundred years old, and it had once been a girl's lycée. All that remained from this period was a tall thin grandfather clock that struck the time loudly, and decorative metal balls on the turns of the banisters. Nine-year-old M surveyed all of this and then went and sat in her classroom, which she liked at this time of the morning, waiting with pleasure for the beginning of the school day. This routine lasted until her class teacher eventually rang home one evening, demanding her mother tell her what was going on in M's homelife and why her daughter came in to school every morning an hour earlier than necessary.

After that M stopped coming to school at such an unearthly hour and even developed the ability to be late and to enjoy being late, but she had a secret, a little agreement she'd made with herself, a kind of compromise—she would set her alarm clock for four or five in the morning, the last hour of darkness when night still felt like an open sea with no further shore, and she would get up straightaway, although she was still half-asleep. Even the radio, which began its daily program at six with the state anthem, was quiet at this time, as if it hadn't yet been invented. Her parents were still asleep, trusting their daughter, who was growing up and becoming more independent. M put her face, creased with sleep like a pillow, under the tap; stuck her toothbrush in tooth powder and fried an egg for herself. She pulled on her woolly tights, the brown school dress and black frilly apron. And when all this was done, and she had fulfilled her duty to the unfriendly world and given everything it demanded of her, M, fully dressed in her uniform and pioneer scarf, slid back into bed, under her quilt, into that familiar sleep-worn space, and slept deeply—until the moment when she couldn't avoid having to roll out into the early gloom.

She had no such tricks up her sleeve on this Sunday morning.

When she'd returned to her room the night before, she hadn't even switched on the light, washing in darkness and groping her way into bed. She was already up and getting ready when the early summer sun appeared.

She left her noisy blue wheeled suitcase behind; she was traveling light from now on. Her possessions, hardly numerous, were laid out on the bedcover to be sorted through.

The following items she decided not to take with her—fate, and the hotel staff, could deal with them as they saw fit.

Her phone, which still hadn't been plugged in, so it couldn't connect with the internet and download all the news, messages and emails that had accumulated. It suddenly looked very large to her, useful now only for looking into, like a dark mirror. She put the charger given to her by the short-haired woman to one side so she wouldn't forget it.

Her own book, in her own language, and the same book in another language with short excerpts marked in pencil, plus two cardboard bookmarks.

A red lacy bra, bought in a fancy shop, intended to cheer her up and make her feel young and shameless.

Almost a whole packet of cigarettes with a picture of an inconsolable family on the front. For some reason she felt she wouldn't need them anymore, and even if this was wishful thinking (both the tall and the short-haired women smoked incessantly, their profession must have predisposed them to it) she'd be better off without them today.

A novel, brought on the journey to distract her, unopened and unread—she'd had other distractions.

The key to the apartment in the house on the lake, with a blue plastic tag on a metal ring.

The keys to the apartment in the city she'd left the year before; there were lots of keys, a whole bunch, and they jangled, bewildered, as she held them up in her fist, then let them go.

A passport with her name, place of birth, and the biometric photograph of a woman, no longer young and with an expression of slightly stunned and unfocused readiness.

A capacious white bag made of leather flayed from a peaceful herbivore, still bearing its scent, the scent of its dreams, of its water and sweat.

A notebook with a silk ribbon bookmark. The calendar pages were densely covered in a variety of notes and scribbles; the rest of the book, where you could write what you wanted, was empty.

A white feather, kept as a souvenir; once fluffed and full, now thin from being kept between pages.

A pair of dressy shoes; though they might still come in handy she had nowhere to go in them.

The piece of paper with the details of the train that the pale-eyed man had given her.

Her name.

She stuffed what she could in a canvas tote with the logo of a big supermarket on it: a second pair of trousers, three changes of underwear (as many as she had) the shirt she hadn't yet worn, her striped toiletry bag. That was it. She thought for another moment and then dropped in a couple of turquoise sweets, just to add something nonessential to her affairs.

Although it was still early, the encouraging aroma of coffee wafted from the breakfast room, and the clattering of cutlery could be heard. She had no appetite at all, it was as if she'd left it behind in the hotel room with her books and the now-lifeless phone. The door closed silently behind her as if it were immaterial and transparent, and she found herself standing in the empty Sunday street. There were no cars or passersby and her light tote bag pressed itself against her, trustingly, without reproach.

Scents came to her in tangled layers on the breeze; a tearful salty wind blew in from the sea; freshly baked rolls in trays awaited mouths; a woman with a scarf around her neck washed a shop window; the scrubbed pavements were free of packaging and pigeon droppings. She walked at a jaunty, almost athletic pace, first down the main street and then through a park along gravel paths, past a pond and a fountain where a tall jet of water swayed, bowing and nodding, although there was no one else around to see it—and we didn't stop to waste time admiring it.

Although there was so much time, she had so much time now and could even, if she wanted, go to the beachfront she hadn't yet visited, in fact it would feel somehow rather apt to dash there and slap a hand down on the seawall, like in a children's race. But why bother?

In the Tarot deck there's another famous card, the meaning of which changes depending on the occasion. It's called, very simply, The Fool, and represents a figure we might once have termed a jester. It should signify new beginnings and new hopes, but alas it's never as straightforward as that. The Fool in his high cap and bells has just set out on his journey and he strides along, eyes wide and mouth open, gazing at everything around him, and is so distracted that he doesn't notice the pitfalls and abysses on all sides. One false move and he could plunge to his death. But he is oblivious, he doesn't yet see the danger, and he also has a sturdy staff, like Peter Cohn; two staffs in fact, one more than strictly necessary. He holds one in his right hand and the other rests on his shoulder, a canvas bundle containing all his possessions tied to it. Off he goes, the Fool—but we don't know where he's going. We might add that he, unlike us, is not alone; he has a creature accompanying him, close at his heels.

If you go through the deck carefully, you'll see that there are only two cards depicting a human sharing their life with an animal and at such close quarters that they seem to be in a sort of conversation with each other. These two are different from the cards that show beasts sitting on the bare earth howling at the moon, or as allegorical beings hidden in the corners, or pulling chariots as faceless and functional horse power. They are the cards where the animals are center stage and can't be ignored, and one of these has the woman who either embraces the lion or restrains him from a rash deed, and the other is the fool: wherever he goes with his bundle he is followed by a little beast, no more than knee-high, probably a dog. It is standing on hind legs and clinging to his trousers, and it isn't clear whether it's about to bite him or is showing him affection. But seemingly we can't do without it: wherever we go the dog is always there, of one flesh with us, an inseparable pair, and when you look at the fool card it's not always clear whether you should see yourself as the one wandering along, without cares or needs, or the one, running behind, sticking as close as it can to the other. It's an unpleasant card, with its wretched vagabond in his cap and bells, and it would be far better to establish a connection with the following card in the sequence: a proper magician or magus laying out his paraphernalia on a folding table and preparing once again to ply his trade. Unfortunately this isn't always possible on the first attempt, and for some it never happens.

As she walked away from the center of town, the desertedness became more charged, ominous, as if the inhabitants had all left the city, abandoning to looters the apartment blocks with their balconies and deckchairs, the trash cans in the yards, the abundant old people's homes and their ancient inhabitants who could no longer be transported from the town. In the window of an old-people's home, an old woman with gray wisps all around her crown stood like a bright curtain, looking out blindly. From here it wasn't far to the turning onto the high road and the fenced-off area with the banners and the big tent. A, as she was now called, shifted the tote bag from one shoulder to the other, quickening her pace. The birds were chirping their indistinct song, and there was no one walking towards her or following her along the streets.

She turned, sure of her way, and looked ahead from her elevated position—but there was nothing there, absolutely nothing. The road was still there of course, as well as the pavement she was walking on, the long white building a good distance ahead, the green slope, and beyond it the trampled waste ground, that barren exhausted stretch of earth where the circus caravan had been stationed. But the trailers, the little tents, even the fence of tarpaulin, were no longer there; it was just a blank space, dumb and vacant. A narrowed her eyes, not yet able to believe it, and trotted down the brown grass of the path towards the waste ground, and the patch of asphalt where the box office had stood, beside the entrance to the tent. There she stopped by the bench, which had been left on its side. The circus was gone.

She had absolutely no idea what had happened, or why Peter Cohn had broken his promise. She would have checked her watch to make sure she wasn't late and had arrived as agreed by seven, a long time before the arranged departure, but she didn't have a watch, she'd become used to checking the time on a screen and now she didn't have a phone either. Still—what difference did it make now? Either she was late, and it was an absurd and irredeemable mistake, or the owner of the circus had decided to move on without her. Or something else had happened and the lions, acrobats and illusionists had all suddenly and mysteriously vanished into thin air, leaving no trail to follow. For our story, none of this matters, and working out what happened, or at what point of the journey the mistake crept in, is now quite impossible.

A dug her heels into the flattened soil and pulled the bench upright so she had something to sit on. Night still lingered in the air. It was cold, and the morning was beginning to assert its presence. They'd left not a scrap of litter, nothing as a farewell or a souvenir—although a few meters from where she was now sitting she saw the old tin can filled with cigarette butts. Grimacing, A stuck her fingers in the can, wiggling them in the ash to find the most smokable butt. Her lighter was still in her pocket—she hadn't managed to relinquish everything in her life after all, and at this precise moment she was thankful. A, first letter of the alphabet, pressed the horrid cigarette end between her lips, breathed in smoke and exhaled. The yellow stray dog with its yellow eyes approached her and sat down in the dust, not too close, but near enough. And the dog thought for a moment, before flopping onto its side, and gazing tactfully past her.

0.

Perhaps the caravan was waiting for them around the corner.

JULY–AUGUST 2023

ACKNOWLEDGMENTS

The author wishes to thank the institutions and people who made this book possible. In the first instance, the hospitality of the Wissenschaftskolleg zu Berlin, where the book was written, especially Barbara Stollberg-Rilinger, Andrea Bergmann, Francisco Martínez Casas.

Work on the book continued at the Columbia Institute for Ideas and Imagination in Paris, with the friendship and support of Mark Mazower and Marie d'Origny. I am endlessly grateful to them for these months.

I must also mention Marie Andersen, thanks to whom the novelist M's journey began, Olga Radetzkaja and our conversation in the Café Obermayer, Katharina Raabe and our walk in the Grunewald, and of course Andrey Kurilkin, Elena Nusinova and Irina Paperno, my first readers.

I am deeply grateful to my English-language publishers, Barbara Epler and Jacques Testard, Tynan Kogane and the editorial staff at Fitzcarraldo Editions and New Directions. My special gratitude to Sasha Dugdale: this book is only a part of a conversation with her that has lasted years.

The translator wishes to thank the Hosking Houses Trust for their generous support, and particularly Sarah Hosking.

I am also very grateful to Don Mee Choi for her hospitality while working on this translation, and to J. O. Morgan for his advice and help. Maria Stepanova has been an unfailing guide and friend to me in all our wanderings.

New Directions Paperbooks—a partial listing

Adonis, Songs of Mihyar the Damascene
César Aira, Ghosts
An Episode in the Life of a Landscape Painter
Ryunosuke Akutagawa, Kappa
Will Alexander, Refractive Africa
Osama Alomar, The Teeth of the Comb
Guillaume Apollinaire, Selected Writings
Jessica Au, Cold Enough for Snow
Paul Auster, The Red Notebook
Ingeborg Bachmann, Malina
Honoré de Balzac, Colonel Chabert
Djuna Barnes, Nightwood
Charles Baudelaire, The Flowers of Evil*
Bei Dao, City Gate, Open Up
Yevgenia Belorusets, Lucky Breaks
Rafael Bernal, His Name Was Death
Mei-Mei Berssenbrugge, Empathy
Max Blecher, Adventures in Immediate Irreality
Jorge Luis Borges, Labyrinths
Seven Nights
Coral Bracho, Firefly Under the Tongue*
Kamau Brathwaite, Ancestors
Anne Carson, Glass, Irony & God
Wrong Norma
Horacio Castellanos Moya, Senselessness
Camilo José Cela, Mazurka for Two Dead Men
Louis-Ferdinand Céline
Death on the Installment Plan
Journey to the End of the Night
Inger Christensen, alphabet
Julio Cortázar, Cronopios and Famas
Jonathan Creasy (ed.), Black Mountain Poems
Robert Creeley, If I Were Writing This
H. D., Selected Poems
Guy Davenport, 7 Greeks
Amparo Dávila, The Houseguest
Osamu Dazai, The Flowers of Buffoonery
No Longer Human
The Setting Sun
Anne de Marcken
It Lasts Forever and Then It's Over
Helen DeWitt, The Last Samurai
Some Trick
José Donoso, The Obscene Bird of Night
Robert Duncan, Selected Poems
Eça de Queirós, The Maias
Juan Emar, Yesterday
William Empson, 7 Types of Ambiguity
Mathias Énard, Compass
Shusaku Endo, Deep River
Jenny Erpenbeck, Go, Went, Gone
Kairos
Lawrence Ferlinghetti
A Coney Island of the Mind
Thalia Field, Personhood
F. Scott Fitzgerald, The Crack-Up
Rivka Galchen, Little Labors
Forrest Gander, Be With
Romain Gary, The Kites
Natalia Ginzburg, The Dry Heart
Henry Green, Concluding
Marlen Haushofer, The Wall
Victor Heringer, The Love of Singular Men
Felisberto Hernández, Piano Stories
Hermann Hesse, Siddhartha
Takashi Hiraide, The Guest Cat
Yoel Hoffmann, Moods
Susan Howe, My Emily Dickinson
Concordance
Bohumil Hrabal, I Served the King of England
Qurratulain Hyder, River of Fire
Sonallah Ibrahim, That Smell
Rachel Ingalls, Mrs. Caliban
Christopher Isherwood, The Berlin Stories
Fleur Jaeggy, Sweet Days of Discipline
Alfred Jarry, Ubu Roi
B. S. Johnson, House Mother Normal
James Joyce, Stephen Hero
Franz Kafka, Amerika: The Man Who Disappeared
Yasunari Kawabata, Dandelions
Mieko Kanai, Mild Vertigo
John Keene, Counternarratives
Kim Hyesoon, Autobiography of Death
Heinrich von Kleist, Michael Kohlhaas
Taeko Kono, Toddler-Hunting
László Krasznahorkai, Satantango
Seiobo There Below
Ágota Kristóf, The Illiterate
Eka Kurniawan, Beauty Is a Wound
Mme. de Lafayette, The Princess of Clèves
Lautréamont, Maldoror
Siegfried Lenz, The German Lesson
Alexander Lernet-Holenia, Count Luna

Denise Levertov, Selected Poems
Li Po, Selected Poems
Clarice Lispector, An Apprenticeship
The Hour of the Star
The Passion According to G. H.
Federico García Lorca, Selected Poems*
Nathaniel Mackey, Splay Anthem
Xavier de Maistre, Voyage Around My Room
Stéphane Mallarmé, Selected Poetry and Prose*
Javier Marías, Your Face Tomorrow (3 volumes)
Bernadette Mayer, Midwinter Day
Carson McCullers, The Member of the Wedding
Fernando Melchor, Hurricane Season
Paradais
Thomas Merton, New Seeds of Contemplation
The Way of Chuang Tzu
Henri Michaux, A Barbarian in Asia
Henry Miller, The Colossus of Maroussi
Big Sur & the Oranges of Hieronymus Bosch
Yukio Mishima, Confessions of a Mask
Death in Midsummer
Eugenio Montale, Selected Poems*
Vladimir Nabokov, Laughter in the Dark
Pablo Neruda, The Captain's Verses*
Love Poems*
Charles Olson, Selected Writings
George Oppen, New Collected Poems
Wilfred Owen, Collected Poems
Hiroko Oyamada, The Hole
José Emilio Pacheco, Battles in the Desert
Michael Palmer, Little Elegies for Sister Satan
Nicanor Parra, Antipoems*
Boris Pasternak, Safe Conduct
Octavio Paz, Poems of Octavio Paz
Victor Pelevin, Omon Ra
Fernando Pessoa
The Complete Works of Alberto Caeiro
Alejandra Pizarnik
Extracting the Stone of Madness
Robert Plunket, My Search for Warren Harding
Ezra Pound, The Cantos
New Selected Poems and Translations
Qian Zhongshu, Fortress Besieged
Raymond Queneau, Exercises in Style
Olga Ravn, The Employees
Herbert Read, The Green Child
Kenneth Rexroth, Selected Poems
Keith Ridgway, A Shock
Rainer Maria Rilke
Poems from the Book of Hours
Arthur Rimbaud, Illuminations*
A Season in Hell and The Drunken Boat*
Evelio Rosero, The Armies
Fran Ross, Oreo
Joseph Roth, The Emperor's Tomb
Raymond Roussel, Locus Solus
Ihara Saikaku, The Life of an Amorous Woman
Nathalie Sarraute, Tropisms
Jean-Paul Sartre, Nausea
Kathryn Scanlan, Kick the Latch
Delmore Schwartz
In Dreams Begin Responsibilities
W. G. Sebald, The Emigrants
The Rings of Saturn
Anne Serre, The Governesses
Patti Smith, Woolgathering
Stevie Smith, Best Poems
Novel on Yellow Paper
Gary Snyder, Turtle Island
Muriel Spark, The Driver's Seat
The Public Image
Maria Stepanova, In Memory of Memory
Wislawa Szymborska, How to Start Writing
Antonio Tabucchi, Pereira Maintains
Junichiro Tanizaki, The Maids
Yoko Tawada, The Emissary
Scattered All over the Earth
Dylan Thomas, A Child's Christmas in Wales
Collected Poems
Thuan, Chinatown
Rosemary Tonks, The Bloater
Tomas Tranströmer, The Great Enigma
Leonid Tsypkin, Summer in Baden-Baden
Tu Fu, Selected Poems
Elio Vittorini, Conversations in Sicily
Rosmarie Waldrop, The Nick of Time
Robert Walser, The Tanners
Eliot Weinberger, An Elemental Thing
Nineteen Ways of Looking at Wang Wei
Nathanael West, The Day of the Locust
Miss Lonelyhearts
Tennessee Williams, The Glass Menagerie
A Streetcar Named Desire
William Carlos Williams, Selected Poems
Alexis Wright, Praiseworthy
Louis Zukofsky, "A"

*BILINGUAL EDITION